PEL AND THE PIRATES

Mark Hebden

Walker and Company
New York

First published in the United States of America
in 1987 by the Walker Publishing Company, Inc.

Library of Congress Cataloging-in-Publication Data

Hebden, Mark, 1916-
    Pel and the pirates.

    I. Title.
PR6058.A6886P455 1987   823'.914   87-2043
ISBN 0-8027-5672-7

Printed in the United States of America

10 9 8 7 6 5 4 3 2 1

1

Death, Evariste Clovis Désiré Pel thought gloomily, surely couldn't be far away. Rigor mortis, he felt certain, was already coursing through his veins. Everything seemed to be dripping wet and he expected to see water rushing in on him at any moment in a vast green flood. In his time he had been close to death on many occasions. He'd been shot at, knocked down, attacked with a variety of blunt or sharp instruments but had somehow managed always to survive. This time he had grave doubts about the outcome, and drowning was a rotten way to go – especially for a newly-promoted detective chief inspector of the Brigade Criminelle of the Police Judiciare on the first day of his honeymoon.

'How do you feel now, Pel?' The question, quiet and steady from Pel's new wife, Geneviève, until recently the Widow Faivre-Perret, made him lift his eyes.

'When do we arrive?' he managed.

'In about another hour?'

Pel's heart sank. Because it had been felt he needed to get as far from police work as possible where he couldn't be called back in an emergency, they had settled for their holiday on the Isle of St. Yves, just the other side of the Ile Boniface, off the south coast of France. Pel had been a little dubious about islands when the idea had been first mooted – he was dubious about anywhere that wasn't within the borders of his beloved Burgundy – and because there was no air link and because in any case Pel was terrified at the thought of flying – they had gone from Nice by boat. Like some wines, Pel didn't travel well and he was now wishing they'd put him in a cannon and fired him across the intervening water in the manner of those acts you saw in circuses. Seafaring vessels, he felt, would be all right so long as they had firm sturdy legs solidly fixed in concrete to the sea bottom.

Famed for its blueness and its calmness, the Mediterranean had surprised him with its greyness and ferocity. He had considered he was doing rather well as they set off. For the first hour there had been no sign of nausea and he had felt that, despite the ominous weather reports, he was not going to embarrass the new Madame Pel by being seasick. No sailor, however, he hadn't allowed for the fact that during the first hour the ferry had been protected from the weather by the Ile Boniface, and as soon as they had rounded the corner and turned broadside on to the wind the roll of the boat had made him realise at once what a child he was in matters of seafaring. Coming from Burgundy, which was about as far as you could get from the sea in Metropolitan France, even a rowing boat was normally almost too much for him. *This* was a monstrous agony, and to make it worse Madame, who had grown up on the coast near La Rochelle, was coping with the roll of the boat with all the aplomb of a pirate.

Pel felt cheated. The previous day, his wedding eve, had been magnificent, windless and with brilliant sunshine, even a cloudless sky so that the waning moon had made the night as light as day. His mind full of romantic thoughts brought on by the brilliance, he had stood in the pocket-handkerchief garden of the house he owned in the Rue Martin-de-Noinville and looked at it for the last time before it went for rent to a lecturer at the university, and thought how his life had changed.

When they returned he would have left the cramped quarters in the Rue Martin-de-Noinville for the new house Madame had acquired at Fontaine, large, furnished with taste, and expensive enough to give Pel, who had never been known as a big spender, nightmares of the first order in case he went bankrupt. Moreover – and this was a triumph indeed – he had finally shuffled off Madame Routy, his housekeeper, who, he considered, was the only bad cook in a country which quite rightly boasted of its culinary expertise.

It seemed to auger well for his future and he had looked forward to a honeymoon in the south, with flowers, blue sky, a millpond sea and a great deal of graceful drinking to quench the thirst that would inevitably come from too much sunshine. But then, on the day of his wedding, the one day when he

2

wished to appear to be gallant, a knight in shining armour, the cursed weather had changed. On the short walk from the Mairie to the church, it had blown his hair – what there was of it – all over his face, and the flight down to Marseilles had been so bumpy it had felt as if their aircraft had been colliding with hard and heavy objects in the sky. Finally, with typical southern treachery – Pel attributed treachery to any part of France that wasn't inside the borders of Burgundy – it had changed completely. The area between Nice and the island of St. Yves, caught in the air currents caused by the mountains behind and the curve of the bay, was as treacherous as the climate round Greece and the appalling weather had inflicted on him this humiliating performance by lashing itself to gale force.

Because the Isle of St. Yves didn't warrant anything bigger, the ferry was only small and, in addition to the few early holiday-makers and the residents of the island who had been on shopping trips to the mainland, the decks were crowded with sacks of potatoes, cartons of produce, engine parts for the ancient machinery that clearly still operated on the island, a crate of chickens, a couple of mournfully-bleating goats, which were probably also suffering from seasickness, and a very old secondhand Citroën Diane.

Because of the variety and amount of the cargo it was impossible to go on deck for a reviving breath of fresh air and everybody on board – including the crew who were sheltering from the weather – was crammed into the tiny saloon where the bar, because of the rolling of the boat, could offer little else but brandy, beer and coffee.

To take his mind off the motion, Pel had tried reading a detective story he had bought from a stand near the ferry jetty, but he didn't like mysteries – they made him feel he knew nothing at all about detection and was totally inadequate compared with the iron-jawed sleuths who peopled them – so he was now trying grimly to read the newspaper. There had been a spectacular shooting in a Nice bar the week before on the 13th. of the month – an unlucky date for someone, obviously – and the newspaper was full of it. Six men standing at the counter had been mown down with a tommy gun. It was clearly a gang crime because Marseilles wasn't far away and everybody knew the reputation of

Marseilles. It stuck out a mile also that people were keeping their mouths shut tight because no weapons had been found and nobody knew who the killers were, despite the fact that they hadn't been wearing masks and the job had been done in daylight. He could imagine a few pursed lips at police headquarters.

The press were suggesting *they* knew, of course. They never did, but they always like to make a lot of song and dance about the private enquiries they were conducting, as if the police didn't know what day it was and needed their help. Always uninhibited about cases which had not yet appeared before the magistrates, they enjoyed pointing the finger. Since it was obviously a gang murder, they were being careful, however, not to point a finger at any of the gangs because that was the surest way there was to a grave in Marseilles harbour wearing a concrete overcoat.

There was also plenty of coverage on an enquiry being held in Paris at that moment into the activities of the Minister for the Bureau of Environmental Surveys. Government funds set aside for the reservation of land and the minerals therein seemed to have been somehow mislaid and the Minister, a junior member of the government, was having to face questions. He seemed bewildered by the whole business, especially since his chief accuser was his deputy, a man called Jean-Jacques Hardy, a handsome politician of some note with a dashing life-style who was regularly seen with attractive women in large cars.

Pel was all for politicians being occasionally put on the hook. Considering it was the only profession in the world where a man couldn't under normal circumstances be sent to jail for losing the firm's money, its good faith or its reputation abroad, he considered they got away lightly, and he was all for seeing one or two put in the dock, if only to encourage the others to behave themselves. This time, however, he wondered if they'd got the wrong man. It was a well-known fact among policemen that the louder a man shouted his innocence the more likely he was to be guilty. The man who swore his innocence on his mother's grave always needed looking into, while the man who swore on the head of his unborn child should be charged within the hour. And while the Minister for Environmental Surveys could produce

4

nothing more than a feeble bleat about his bewilderment, Jean-Jacques Hardy was loudly claiming to have no knowledge whatsoever of what had been going on.

Instinctively, Pel didn't like Jean-Jacques Hardy. For a start, he was too good-looking, and that was always a black mark with Pel, who wasn't, and in addition he represented a district in the Vendée, which was also enough in itself to darken him in Pel's eyes. As a young sergeant he had once been obliged to spend a whole month in the north-west of the Vendée, and its flat marshy land, its winding roads, its dykes, its empty horizons and its rows of stark telegraph poles had put him off it for ever. No wonder, he had thought at the time, that when France had produced a revolution against the Bourbons in 1789 the people of the Vendée had produced a counter-revolution against it. They were the thoughts of a bigot, he knew, but he often felt the world had room for a few more bigots.

The vessel lurched heavily, lifting slowly and ominously before dropping into the trough between two waves like a high-speed lift going down the shaft of a skyscraper. It left Pel's stomach suspended somewhere in the region of his throat so that he lowered the paper hurriedly. Surely, he thought miserably, he wasn't going to disgrace himself on the first day of his married life by being sick?

'How do you feel, Pel?'

Since becoming engaged, Madame had suddenly taken to addressing him by his surname, not through any lack of affection but because, she claimed, she found it a little awesome being part of the life of someone with the sort of reputation her new husband bore. There was another reason, too, which Pel suspected was probably more applicable. Simply that she found his Christian names just too much to swallow. Evariste, Clovis and Désiré were all of them all very well on their own but together they were just too much. Pel's mother had had ambitions for her son – nothing much, perhaps the presidency of the Republic and a wife who was a famous film star – and had decided he should have the names to go with them. Unfortunately, she had been just *too* ambitious and Pel had settled for being a cop, anyway.

Not daring to speak, he cranked his head round and pulled a face.

5

'Try closing your eyes,' Madame suggested. 'Don't look through the portholes. Just think of pleasant things.'

Pel thought about being married, which promised to be the pleasantest thing that had ever happened in what he considered, in his pessimistic, gloom-orientated manner, to be a long life full of woes. With Inspector Darcy, his second-in-command as best man, the ceremony had taken place that morning at the Mairie of Fontaine, and had been blessed at the Church of St. Michel nearby. A noisy reception had followed with jokes by the Chief, then the newly-wedded couple had driven to the airport in a procession of cars decorated with ribbons and flowers, all playing hell with the traffic as they pumped at their horns – Frenchmen always liked to let people know they'd been to a wedding. At Nice, they had taken a taxi to the port and, not without difficulty because it was small and unimportant, had found the ferry to the Ile de St. Yves.

By this time, Pel was beginning to regret the whole thing and was wishing he had stayed safely in his house in the Rue Martin-de-Noinville. Although no bigger than a dog's kennel, desperately needing paint and looking inside as if it had been papered with wrapping paper, at least it didn't go up and down. Perhaps, he felt gloomily, he had been too precipitate in stepping outside his league to get married and it was God's judgment on him.

'How do you feel now?' Madame Pel asked, laying a soft hand on his.

'A little better,' he said, not really believing it. A flood of embarrassment and shame swept over him. 'I can't imagine what you see in a husband who gets seasick on a sea like a millpond.'

'*I* wouldn't call it like a mill pond,' Madame reassured him. 'It looks like a typhoon to me, though I don't suppose it is, and I see a great deal more in you than you ever see in yourself.'

It was pleasant, Pel reflected, to be informed that there were more attractive facets to your character than you'd thought – because for the life of him, over the years as he'd looked in his mirror as he shaved, he'd never been able to see what people saw in him: he personally wouldn't have given him house room.

6

'After all,' she went on – and he couldn't help wondering how much she was just trying to make him feel better – 'you're successful. You're a chief inspector at an age when most people haven't even got to inspector. You're brave. I know that because of the time you risked your life to save Sergeant Misset.'

It might have been better if he hadn't, Pel thought to himself. Lazy, shifty and unreliable, Misset was no adornment to Pel's squad.

'You're also honest and very much kinder than you realise.'

'I am?'

'Claudie Darel told me of your many kindnesses' – Claudie Darel, who was the only female member of his team, must like him a lot better than he realised ' – and you're fair. You don't claim credit for yourself when it's your team who've done the work.'

'She told you that?'

'And a lot more. As did Darcy and Nosjean and De Troquereau. Even the Chief and Judge Polverari.'

Tiens, Pel thought, the wonder of it! All his life he had thought what a sour-faced grouch he was and here were people finding him quite bearable. He was going to have a hell of a job living up to it.

'And that,' Madame went on firmly, 'is only part of it. I have my own special reasons, of course. I see things in you that other people don't.'

Such as being seasick, Pel decided as the boat gave another lurch. Such as being tight with his money. Such as being nervous of Madame Routy. And she still hadn't seen him first thing in the morning with a day's growth of beard, his hair on end, and dark blue hollows under his eyes that made him look like a giant panda.

She was studying the sea beyond the portholes now. 'We've rounded the corner,' she announced. 'We're in the shelter of St. Yves. It's calmer now.'

Pel found it hard to believe.

'Any moment we'll be there.'

To his surprise they were. Within ten minutes the motion of the boat had eased and, opening his eyes warily, he found they were in a small landlocked harbour with white houses round it.

'Is the house we've taken here?' he asked.

'No. I took one called the Villa des Roses near the harbour of Biz. It's a small town just to the north. The travel agent here recommended it. He thought we'd prefer to be away from everybody else. This place's the Vieux Port.'

Pel nodded. It made sense, he had to admit. He had no idea what sort of orgies people indulged in on their honeymoons but he had a feeling that, as far as he was concerned, it might *well* be better to be away from everybody else; and they had decided on a house instead of a hotel because, they had felt, neither of them being in the first flush of youth, that setting up house on holiday might give them time to grow used to each other. Especially, Pel thought, early in the morning when he was inclined to regard the world through dark-brown tinted spectacles.

The boat was swinging into the bay now. At one side the place had been modernised and there was a great deal of concrete, with jetties, tall posts bearing lights, and a concrete harbour-master's office. Beyond was an expanse as big as the Parc des Princes covered with gaudy, plastic-seated chairs in neat rows. Because of the weather the chairs were all unoccupied but half the population of the town seemed to be standing on the terrasses of the little bars that surrounded them, backs against the wall out of the wind to watch the ferry arrive, all in shirts, blue trousers and a sort of rope-soled canvas-topped shoe.

As the ferry turned to head for the jetty, it was passed by another boat, a huge glittering launch moving at full speed for the shelter of the harbour. The wash it created set the ferry rolling and Pel's stomach curvetting like an unbroken foal.

'The Vicomte's,' a man alongside him said. 'They always come in like that.'

He lit a cigarette and blew the smoke into Pel's face, reminding him of the incredible fact that, due to his nausea, he hadn't smoked since they had left the mainland. The way he was feeling now, he was sure, a cigarette would restore not only his health but his peace of mind. Giving his new wife a shifty glance and seeing she was looking in the other direction, he sneaked one out with the urgency of a man in the desert deprived of water and, sucking the smoke down to

8

his socks, had the pleasure of blowing it into the face of the man alongside him next time he turned to sound off about the island.

The big launch was mooring up alongside one of the concrete jetties now and immediately a lorry carrying petrol drew up, as if ordered by radio, a pipe was run aboard, and a man started up a pump.

'Always fuels up the minute he comes in,' Pel's informant went on. 'It's the only bowser on the island and it's private. The rest of us have to fill our cars from cans. It's so he can take off again for anywhere he fancies at a moment's notice. What a way to live! Consorting with the mighty. All those Greek shipping tycoons, all those jet set Americans from Monte Carlo. I wouldn't mind a life like that.' He glanced at Pel. 'You feeling better, my friend? You looked rough back there.'

Pel scowled, not liking to be reminded what a rotten sailor he was.

'André's the name,' the man said, offering his hand. 'Luigi André. I live here. I run the restaurant at Le Havre du Sud. *Luigi's*. I'm Luigi. It's the best restaurant on the island. You on holiday?'

'That's the general idea,' Pel admitted.

'Come and see me. I'll remember you. Never forget a face. I'll give you the best meal you ever ate.'

The very thought of food made Pel feel ill and he wished Luigi André would go away.

But he didn't. He was gesturing at the big launch. 'Too many of that type round here,' he said. 'In summer they come in hordes. People with money, most of it dishonestly earned.'

Pel's instincts were aroused, even through his nausea. 'Did the Vicomte earn his money dishonestly?'

André shrugged. 'He inherited it. Which is just as bad.'

'Was he responsible – ' Pel's hand gestured at the new concrete of the square and the harbour ' – for all this?'

André shrugged. 'That was a consortium. Financiers. They get into everything. They've got into our island and they're behind all the building and speculating that goes on here. A type who lives at the other side of the island runs it. Nobody wanted it but nobody else has the money to oppose him, so he got away with it. New harbour when we didn't want one, new development at Muriel, the big hotel here. Holiday homes, people building and buying old houses to convert. Mind you, they've taken a knock in the last year. Somebody's been going round setting fire to them. Especially lately.'

'Oh? Why?'

'Nationalism. *Our* brand of nationalism, I suppose you'd call it. Youngsters on the island can't compete with people from Marseilles and Nice and the result is that prices go up beyond what they can pay and somebody's decided it might be a good idea to frighten them off.'

The afternoon was already finished and the dusk was approaching. The heavily-wooded hills lifting behind the harbour looked dark and ominous and the whole town, thriftily avoiding switching on its lights too soon in the manner of many Mediterranean communities where for some strange reason a 40-watt bulb was often considered sufficient to light a ballroom, looked gloomy, depressing and ominous.

'It looks,' Pel observed with a profound and rooted pessimism, 'as though things go on here that don't bear talking about.'

He didn't know the half of it.

2

The ferry had dropped an anchor and was now swinging round it to put its flat rear end against the quay. Ropes were flung and the vessel tilted as everyone crowded to one side, anxious to be shot of it.

'A taxi meets us,' Madame announced. 'It takes us direct to Biz and the Villa des Roses. We don't have to worry about a thing. Everything's laid on. They leave a hamper of food and wine for us for the first night, and tomorrow we do our own shopping. We've never shopped together before.'

Despite the obvious eagerness of everybody to be clear of the wretched, diesel-smelling little ferry, they had to wait a good half hour until the sacks and cartons, the crate of chickens, the goat, the old Diane and all the rest of the cargo were removed from the deck to allow them ashore, then, assisted by brown, knotted hands, they tight-roped across a narrow plank to the quay. As he stepped on to the ancient stones, Pel breathed a sigh of relief.

A policeman was standing on the jetty near a row of coloured boats drawn up on the slip. He looked overweight and shabby and André snorted.

'Cops,' he said.

'Don't you like cops?' Pel asked.

'Look at him. Would *you*? I know police. Whenever they're in Le Havre du Sud, they drop into my restaurant, expecting a drink or something to eat. A coffee at the very least. They have the energy of a sloth and the sparkle of a pile of sand. It's no wonder we remain in the backwaters of the last century.'

'*Do* you remain in the backwaters of the last century?'

'One man runs this island.'

'The Vicomte?'

Luigi slapped Pel on the back. It was like being hit by a

11

swinging girder and made him almost swallow his cigarette. 'You are learning, Monsieur,' he said.

Sure enough, there *was* a taxi to meet them. But it was so old, Pel was convinced it had seen service in the Franco-Prussian War. At the very least, it was one of the Taxis of the Marne.

It was rusty, minus a front wing – complete with headlamp – and the lid of the boot was held down with string. There was no bumper on the back and the tyres were worn as smooth as a child's balloon. The driver, who took their luggage, seemed nervous and fumbled the suitcases, dropping one to Madame's alarm – because she'd bought it new for her honeymoon. He didn't seem to have his eyes on what he was doing, in fact, and kept staring towards a group of men standing with their backs to a nearby bar out of the wind. Above their heads someone had used an aerosol can to paint a slogan. *Save food. Eat tourists.* It seemed to reflect the weather, the expressionless stares of the watching men, and the hostile attitude of the islanders to the people who cluttered up their towns and villages every summer.

'You'll soon be there,' the driver said. 'The agents are waiting for you. You'll like it. On a promontory. Beautiful view of the sea on both sides. Own beach. Everything you need. If you need transport, just ask for me. Paolo Caceolari. I'm from Nice originally. Lived on the Promenade des Anglais.'

Pel didn't believe him for a minute. 'Can't we hire a car?' he asked.

'Very difficult,' Caceolari said. 'They have to bring them over specially from the mainland. Ask the agents. I think they brought one over today. It's better to ask for me. My charges are very low. You can put them down as expenses. You'll know how. You'll be a businessman, I expect. We get a lot of those.'

'My husband,' Madame said proudly, 'is a policeman. And a very good one, too. He's Chief Inspector Pel. You may have heard of him.'

'Pel?' Caceolari wrinkled his brows. 'I've heard that name. That case of those murdered cops.'

'One of my husband's cases.' To Pel's surprise, Madame really did sound proud.

Caceolari looked pleased to make their acquaintance. 'I read it,' he said. 'It was in all the papers. Good cops are what we could do with here.'

'Oh?' Pel's professional interest was again roused and his intelligence clicked into gear. 'Why?'

Caceolari pushed them into the rear of the car. The seat had collapsed and was so low they had to crane their necks to see out. 'Things happen,' he said.

'What sort of things?'

'Well – just things. I – '

'Yes?'

'Nothing.'

Pel's curiosity was caught. He had listened to so many people answering questions and making confessions, he instinctively knew Caceolari would have liked to tell him something.

But Caceolari was clearly nervous and kept his head down. Scrambling into his seat, he tried the starter and when it didn't work, automatically – as if they'd expected it wouldn't work – the half dozen men leaning on the wall gave the car a shove. Caceolari gave them a worried look but when the car was rolling along, he put it into gear and the engine started.

'Ecco!' he said. 'Voilà! She goes.'

The drive from the Vieux Port to Biz and the Villa des Roses was by way of roughly-made roads full of hairpin turns, precipitous hills and narrow corners, on more than one of which they had to wait for the passage of some late-moving cartload of farm produce, while Caceolari, the taximan, put his head through the window and yelled abuse which was as much ignored by the drivers as by the mules pulling the carts.

By the time they reached the Villa des Roses it was raining and dark. Caceolari stopped alongside a dry-stone wall in the shade of a group of olive trees overlooking the sea. There was another car there, a large gleaming Peugeot. Climbing out, Pel stared about him.

'Where's the house?' he asked.

'Down there.'

Caceolari pointed down a steep slope of scree and stone and in the darkness Pel could just see a roof and a few lights.

'Can't you drive down there?'

13

'Not possible. Too steep.' Caceolari paused. 'It's a pity you can't – '

'Can't what?'

'Well, nothing gets done and – well – ' Caceolari shrugged. 'Anyway, it's nothing.'

Pel was intrigued. The taxi driver was clearly eager to involve him in something, but again he changed his mind and stuffing suitcases under his arms, began to head down the slope. Standing in the open doorway of the villa, which looked attractive with its lights, gay orange-coloured covers and a bowl of flowers, were a man and a woman. They looked colourful, handsome and well-fed and they wore the shirts and trousers and the rope-soled, canvas-topped shoes everybody on the island seemed to wear.

'Pierre and Josephine Dupont,' the man said, smiling. 'Agents for the owner. Our office is by the harbour in the Vieux Port. Welcome to St. Yves.'

As Caceolari brought in the rest of the baggage, the house seemed roomy and warm-looking. It was built round two sides of a small courtyard, the other two sides occupied by raised rockeries covered with flowers, shrubs and small cactus-like plants. The Duponts explained how things worked, how they had to be sparing with water when taking a bath, and how they shouldn't be alarmed if the electricity went off.

'After all,' Dupont said, 'this is a small island and we have neither the equipment nor the expertise of the mainland. It soon comes on again.'

They took their leave with surprising speed and the new Monsieur and Madame Pel were left on their own. Madame held out her arms and for a moment or two they clutched each other, pleased at last to be alone. Then Madame pushed away her husband, business-like and efficient.

'I expect you're hungry,' she said. 'We'd better find the hamper and make a meal.'

But the 'hamper' consisted of a tin of meat, some very fatty ham, a loaf, six tomatoes, a lettuce, and a bottle of very indifferent white wine which Pel, a Burgundian to the core, was disgusted to notice came from somewhere he'd never heard of.

'Tomorrow,' he promised darkly, 'I shall want to see Monsieur Dupont.'

However, with the bottle of wine and some food inside them they felt better and Pel began to wonder what the fishing was like. After a while Madame suggested she could do with a bath and bed. But the bedrooms, which were in the other wing of the house, could not be reached, they discovered, except along the verandah – something which could present problems if it rained hard. Moreover the bed appeared to be damp.

'I suppose – 'Madame was trying hard to make the best of things ' – that, being early in the year, nothing's aired yet.' She managed a smile. 'We'll have to keep each other warm.'

The bath turned out to be a shower, set for some reason waist-high in the wall so that you had to kneel on the floor, and the water pressure was so indifferent it seemed easier to fill a large bowl and stand in it.

'This,' Madame Pel said, 'is not my idea of a good villa.'

In that Pel was certainly in agreement but, since Madame had done the booking, he was anxious to please and be encouraging. 'How were you to know?' he said. 'It'll seem much better in daylight.'

It was almost midnight now and the rain was easing off, but Pel was smoking as if his life depended on it. Despite the terror of cancer, asthma and all the other diseases attendant on a weak will, he had never been able to drop the habit. He had managed to cut it down – 'A million a day,' he claimed, 'to five hundred thousand' – but at the moment he seemed to be attempting to make up for lost time because they had found other faults with the Villa des Roses. The promontory on which it was built, which gave them the boasted views in two directions, also enabled them to catch every breath of wind that came and at the moment it was blowing half a gale. And, Pel decided, someone hadn't done their homework properly on the drawing board because the house had been built too near the edge of the sea and the hillside seemed to have slipped a little so that there was a huge crack in one wall, and brand-new concrete buttresses which suggested that the owner, terrified of the place dropping on to the rocks below, had done a last-minute shoring-up job. Finally there didn't seem to be a rose bush within sight.

15

By this time, he was in a bad temper and only Madame's sunny disposition, which seemed to be untouched despite the disappointments, stopped him finding a heavy blunt instrument and setting off there and then in search of the Duponts. Indeed, it was only as Madame went to sort out the bathing facilities, that he discovered that none of the doors and windows, which had stood invitingly open when they had arrived, would shut. They were not only warped with the subsidence or the winter damp but they also possessed broken locks. Sourly, he found a heavy stone with which to hold the salon door closed and a piece of string with which to secure the bedroom windows. This, he decided, was something they must never learn at the Hôtel de Police back home. While the occupants of that establishment respected Pel's skill as a detective and were wary of the cutting edge of his temper, the disasters of his private life were often subject to a great deal of merriment. Having seen Madame, they had grudgingly admitted that there must be more to him than met the eye but a story like this would destroy the image as surely as if he had lost his trousers while climbing into the wedding car.

When Madame reappeared, wearing slippers and a housecoat, Pel saw her to the bedroom and explained the workings of the attachments he had found, then left her attending to her hair and face, while he headed for the bathroom. He banged his elbow on the door, slipped on the soapy floor and cracked his knee on the shower, and as the night grew cooler, ended up half-frozen and shivering. Normally as warm-blooded as a frog, even a hint of chill in the air was enough to leave him petrified, so, because he liked to believe he took exercise, he did a few gentle callisthenics to warm himself up. Since he was also afraid that too much vigorous exercise might give him a heart attack, they were so mild as to be virtually non-existent and consisted chiefly of half a dozen knee-bends, a few moments of wild flapping of his arms and a lot of violent puffing. As he brushed his hair, he studied himself in the mirror. Not bad for a man of his age, he decided. On the other hand, he had to admit, decidedly not very good either. Doggedly brushing his teeth, he headed for the bedroom. The trip across the courtyard was enough to chill him to the marrow.

The door was ajar and Madame was sitting up in bed, holding a book. As nervous as a lion-tamer going solo for the first time, Pel gave her a smile which was intended to be tender but came out like a death's head grin. She put down her book and smiled back at him with surprising confidence. Pel removed his dressing gown and slippers with deliberation. He was desperately proud of his new wife, and, indeed, proud of himself that he'd managed to acquire such an attractive partner. Sitting up in bed, Madame didn't seem much bigger than a child saying her catechism, small-framed and, now that she'd taken off her spectacles, large-eyed in the feeble light. Perhaps it would be all right after all, he thought. She was a touch short-sighted and, without her glasses, he probably managed to look like Superman.

This, he decided, was a watershed in his life. His wife seemed nothing like as nervous as he was. After all, he thought, she was a widow and, having been through it all before, doubtless knew how to handle the situation. He drew a deep breath and was just heading for the bed, when he heard a squeal of brakes nearby then a yell just outside. As he swung round sharply, he heard running feet and something sliding down the steep stone-and-scree slope that led to the house.

Swearing under his breath, he turned to the door. Why did God have it in for him so? Not even on his wedding night was he going to be blessed with peace. Some drunk from the village was coming to create an uproar and disturb the emotional balance – delicate enough on any honeymoon, on Pel's positively hair-trigger. He had been hoping against hope that for once in his life he would acquit himself well but he couldn't imagine such a possibility with a horde of lunatics outside yelling their heads off.

The slithering footsteps stopped and they heard a thump, as if someone had fallen, and the sound of moaning. For a moment, Pel and his wife looked at each other in silence then Pel peered through the slats in the ventilator set in the door. He knew he ought to go and investigate, but he was seething with anger at the prospect.

'Do take care!'

The way Pel felt at that moment, he thought, it was the intruder who would have to take care. He'd brought his pistol

17

with him, as he always did, and he had a feeling that if it had been handy he might even have shot him.

He opened the door and peered out. The sky had cleared and in the light of the waning moon, he saw a man lying on his face at the bottom of the slope, his arms outspread, his head in shadow. With Madame, once more hurriedly clothed in her housecoat, peering out behind him, Pel stepped outside. The wind from the sea hit him like a knife.

Moving warily to the unconscious figure, he bent down and touched it, ready for tricks. He'd heard of idiots who made a wedding night chaos with their antics and it was just possible, despite their efforts to prevent it, that someone on the island had learned about their new estate. For a moment even, he wondered if one of his team had put them up to it. But, no, they wouldn't dare. They knew Pel's temper too well, though there was always Sergeant Misset, who was a fool. With his own marriage rapidly heading for the rocks, Misset liked to pester the girls in the typing pool at the Hôtel de Police and it was just possible *he* might consider it joke enough to pay someone to disrupt Pel's honeymoon.

But, as the light from the door fell on the silent figure, he saw it was Caceolari, the taxi driver. He was dressed, as they'd last seen him when he'd brought them to the Villa des Roses, in shirt and trousers and rope-soled shoes, and there was a spreading stain on his back. Staring down, Pel realised that his own hands where he'd touched him were red and shining.

'Open that door wider!'

There was an unexpected briskness in his voice and Madame didn't hesitate. She had already learned that Pel engaged on police business was a very different man from the Pel who had nervously wooed and married her. Pel was a split personality every bit of the way, uncertain in his private life but more than confident in his professional one. She jerked the door wide and it was then that Pel saw that Caceolari's shirt was soaked with blood.

'Better find a towel,' he said. 'Something to use as a swab. He must have fallen down the slope. He's badly hurt.'

Madame was just heading for the kitchen as Pel started to turn Caceolari on to his back. What he saw made him catch his breath and he held up his hand, stopping Madame in her tracks.

'Don't bother,' he said. Someone had attacked Caceolari and they had made no mistake. There was a deep wound in his chest and he was already quite dead.

3

The courtyard was filled with people. The story had got around quickly and at the top of the hill more people were standing with their mouths open, taking everything in. There were always people at the scene of a crime. They'd have appeared, Pel decided, if it had been committed in outer space.

Policemen were standing in a group near the body. Their uniforms were shabby and their belts and buttons unpolished. Two of them at least looked as though they hadn't shaved and one of them was toying with his gun, which, even at a distance, looked to Pel as if it was inclined to be rusty. A doctor was bent over the body. He wore a straw hat on the back of his head and from beneath it fell long grey straggly hair that looked none too clean. His suit was unpressed and creased and the cuffs were frayed; on his feet he wore the canvas-topped shoes that everybody on the island wore. The whole bunch of them looked a little unsavoury and it seemed to Pel that they needed a good sergeant-major to liven them up.

Surprisingly unterrified by all that had happened, Madame was in the kitchen making coffee for everyone, while Pel himself watched from the sidelines, missing nothing. At first he had been regarded with suspicion by the police as just another interfering holidaymaker who doubtless made a habit of slaughtering taxi drivers for fun, but later, when they had demanded his papers and his identity had become known, with some reverence as a man who had forgotten more about crime than the locals would learn in a lifetime.

When it had finally dawned on him what had happened, it had occurred to him that the obvious thing to do was call the police, but there was no telephone and he could hardly leave his new wife alone in a house where the doors didn't

20

lock properly when there might well be a criminal lunatic prowling around. In the end, his gun hurriedly stuffed into his pocket, they had set off together up the slope where, within a few hundred yards, hidden among the olives, they had discovered the cottage of a smallholder called Murati surrounded by chicken runs and garden.

It had taken a long time to get the police because the Muratis' old van didn't work and Pel had forbidden Murati to touch Caceolari's battered vehicle, which was standing outside, in case it carried fingerprints. As Murati had finally departed – none too willingly – on a bicycle, his wife had ushered the Pels into the kitchen where she had produced a bottle of brandy and offered it round. The interior of the house was small and very ugly, with all the chrome fittings peasants loved so much, but at least Madame Pel was safe there, and after helping himself to the bottle even Pel began to feel happier and managed to slip away to prowl round the grounds. He found nothing and when the police arrived, everybody, including Madame, returned down the slope to the greater space and comfort of the Villa des Roses.

The police on the island were administered by a brigadier called Beauregard, who was obsequious, overweight, crafty-looking and, like his men, seemed as though he never stood close enough to his razor. At that moment, he was staring down at the body. 'Il a cassé sa pipe,' he observed to the doctor. 'Kicked the bucket all right.'

The doctor looked up. He had a face that looked as if he'd been wearing it a long time and it was becoming a little threadbare. 'I'd have said that was fairly obvious,' he said tartly. 'Who did it?'

'God only knows.'

The doctor gave the brigadier a sour look. 'I knew we had some important people on this island,' he said, 'but I didn't know they were as important as *that*.'

As the brigadier and the doctor talked, Pel studied the Villa des Roses. It was clearly a fraud. The electricity had twice failed for an hour and the machinery which worked the pump in the well below the property had broken down so that all the water for the coffee was being transported from the smallholder's place up the scree slope. Now that it was daylight, Pel noticed also that the gutterings were falling off

21

and the one on the end of the building, he could see, would in a heavy rainstorm direct its contents straight into the bedroom, while, since all the rainwater would run off the slopes down the hill, the courtyard itself would inevitably be flooded and in turn flood the house. Obviously the place had been built in a hurry by a one-armed bricklayer and a boy with a fretsaw, and while it might suffice for hot weather it certainly wouldn't do when it rained or the wind blew. In addition, the private beach which had been advertised turned out to be a narrow-gutted oil-covered inlet into the cliffs filled with small boulders on which it would be quite impossible to lie or even sit down in the sun, and, as Pel had discovered while searching round the place for any signs of who it was who had killed Caceolari, it could only be reached by a hair-raising climb down a narrow path overhanging the cliff.

The police were still talking with the doctor as he sat on the verandah and drank a cup of coffee. The affair was none of his business and he was quite happy to leave it to someone else.

'What shall we do?' he asked his wife. 'Go home?'

'Oh, no!' Madame was far less frightened than he'd expected her to be. 'We're on our honeymoon.'

'Well, we can't stay here. Even if we wanted to, the police wouldn't let us. They'll seal the place up.'

'Perhaps we can find somewhere else. This place's hopeless anyway. It's my fault entirely.'

He took her hand and kissed it. Pel could be gallant with Madame even if he couldn't with anybody else.

'We could perhaps find a hotel,' he suggested. 'I'll get a taxi – '

'Unless that poor man's taxi was the only one on the island. It might well have been. And I'd still rather have a house. It won't be difficult. The season hasn't started. We'll see the Duponts. They'll fix something.'

'They'd better,' Pel said darkly. 'And we'd better settle for somewhere in the village. I've just discovered that this place is two kilometres outside. You go along the cliffs, climb down a path which, I gather, is infested with adders, cross the beach, climb the other side, then walk along the road. Without a car it would take half an hour and we'd have

22

to carry everything we ate or drank. And wine,' he added thoughtfully, 'is heavy.'

After a while, the brigadier disappeared. When he returned he was accompanied by a tall slender man who was immaculately dressed in a way that reminded Pel of an aristocrat prepared for the guillotine. He wore a silk scarf at his throat as if it were a cravat, and his shirt cuffs were frilled. From them emerged wrists so slight they looked barely strong enough to lift a cup of coffee. His neck was the same, stalklike, supporting a large head which consisted of narrow cheeks, penetrating blue eyes and a large beak of a nose. The grey hair that surrounded it was over-long and seemed to have been artificially waved. Like everybody else, he wore the canvas rope-soled slippers.

Brigadier Beauregard, shifty-looking as ever, approached Pel. 'We've a request to put to you, sir,' he said.

'Oh? What's that?'

'We thought you'd like to take over the case.'

Pel was startled. Recovering, he glared at the sergeant. 'You've got another think coming,' he said coldly.

Beauregard shrugged. 'Well, there's no detective force on this island. Just me and five men. That's all. We decided – '

'Who decided?' Pel snapped.

'I did,' the man behind Beauregard said.

'And who're you?'

'I am the authority on this island. Prosecutor, judge, jury, lawmaker. Everything.' The tall man held out his hand. 'I'm the Vicomte de la Rochemare. I own the island. I have a place over the hill, overlooking the Vieux Port where you doubtless arrived. When the brigadier's in a dilemma he comes to me.'

'Then,' Pel said shortly, 'you'd better think again. I have my wife here with me. I can't just abandon her. Besides,' he added as an afterthought, 'I had intended to do a little fishing.'

'I fear you'll have to forget it for a little, Chief Inspector.' Rochemare held out a telegram form. 'I telephoned the Chief of Police in Nice who agreed to telephone your own Chief of Police, who agreed half an hour ago that we should have the benefit of your skill. This is proof in the form of a telegram.'

23

Pel almost snatched the piece of paper. He saw his own name and that of the Chief. He looked up at Rochemare. If looks could have killed, Rochemare would have dropped dead on the spot.

'I've just got married,' Pel snarled. 'I'm on my honeymoon.'

Rochemare became all apologies at once, 'I had no idea, of course,' he said.

Somehow, Pel didn't believe him. A man who obviously had a finger in every pie on the island would have known not only his identity within minutes of him landing but also why he was there. Vicomte or no vicomte, he made his feelings very clear and demanded to speak to his Chief.

'But of course, of course.' The Vicomte gestured at Beauregard. 'Arrange for the Chief Inspector to use the telephone.'

Pel glared. It was a damned odd set-up, he thought, when a brigadier of police, a sergeant no less, took his orders from a civilian.

While Rochemare graciously agreed to take coffee with Madame Pel, Pel and Beauregard stamped up the scree slope to the Muratis' house. Beauregard didn't beat about the bush.

'We want to use your telephone to get in touch with the mainland,' he said.

Murati looked alarmed. 'Why not use your own?'

'Because – ' Beauregard leaned over him ' – because it's too far away. That's why.'

'But the mainland! That'll be expensive. Who's going to pay? The police?'

'Rochemare's paying. He sent us.'

Murati still looked unhappy but it was obvious that Rochemare's word was law on St. Yves.

The telephone was in the kitchen and they had to remove the carcass of a chicken Madame Murati had been plucking, feathers, dirty plates, and a cat which was sleeping on the telephone wire. Beauregard asked for the operator and gave instructions. Not a number, Pel noticed, just instructions.

'And look slippy,' he said. 'The Vicomte's in this.'

He slammed the telephone back. 'She'll ring back,' he announced.

As they waited, he turned to Pel. 'I knew a Pel once, Chief,' he said. 'He was a policeman, too. Avignon, I think it was.'

Pel didn't like people relating him to other policemen. He felt he was unique. 'Sure it wasn't Aix?' he asked.

'That's it, Chief! Aix.'

'Sacked for corruption,' Pel said shortly. 'Got away with half a million francs. Had an "in" on half the bordels in the city.'

Beauregard's expression didn't alter. 'The Vicomte's all right,' he said encouragingly.

Pel said nothing. He wasn't often involved with the gratin but he felt he could handle them.

'Family came from Aquitaine.'

Pel ignored the observation. In Aquitaine the upper crust talked a lot about Queen Eleanor who'd married Henry of Anjou who became King of England, and even tried to pretend to be related. They gave their dogs English names, claimed to know the Kennedys and the Onassis family and sent their children to English universities for their accents.

The telephone call was slow coming through so they used the time to question Murati and his wife. They hadn't heard a thing they considered at all unusual. Just the braking of a car and shortly afterwards a second. Then they'd heard shouts and one of the cars had started up and left in a hurry. Thinking that perhaps the new occupants of the Villa des Roses were having visitors, they had taken no notice because holidaymakers often had noisy parties and they'd not realised what had been happening until they'd been wakened by Pel.

The telephone rang. It was the Chief. Considering him guilty of the basest treachery, Pel let him have it loud and clear. The Chief listened silently then he asked quietly, 'What does your wife say?'

Pel stopped in mid-tirade. 'I haven't asked her,' he admitted.

'Perhaps you'd better. If she has no objections, I can't see why *you* have.'

Pel suddenly wondered if the Chief had known his wife before he had, but he dismissed the thought quickly.

'We've had this request through Nice,' the Chief went on. 'They're fully occupied. Six murders in one go. You'll have read about them. That's enough to fill anybody's day. And since you're there, they thought you might be able to sort things out before the trail goes cold.'

'I'm supposed to be here for a fortnight,' Pel snorted. 'What happens if it takes longer?'

'Darcy can hold the fort here. We can doubtless arrange something. It won't come off your leave, so in effect it'll be an extra holiday with pay, won't it?'

'A working holiday,' Pel snapped. 'And there'll have to be a few arrangements made here for our comfort.'

'See that they're made. If they want you, they've got to make things easy. If they don't, you up sticks and come home. You've got the sort of reputation these days that allows you to behave like a prima ballerina.'

Pel's eyebrows shot up. A modest but ambitious man, he hadn't realised he'd become that well known. Perhaps he'd do well to avoid embittering his declining years with too many signs of disapproval.

'See that Nice gives you all the help you need,' the Chief insisted. 'They'll pay all expenses with this Vicomte de la Rochemare, of course. He made the request.'

A little dazed to find he was important enough for VIP treatment, Pel returned to the Villa des Roses. The Vicomte and Madame Pel were busy with coffee, though as the door opened the Vicomte was holding Madame's hand and leaning forward in a way that suggested he was practised at all the social arts. Doubtless, Pel decided, he was an accomplished seducer and obviously he didn't consider he'd overstepped the mark because he didn't let go in a hurry, while Madame clearly found his charm to her taste and didn't seem to find anything odd about it.

Pel announced stiffly what had happened and agreed that it might be possible if his wife agreed. Rochemare was all apologies and smiles.

'I very much regret the inconvenience,' he said. 'Especially since you'll not have the advantage of the normal police equipment you're used to.'

'Police equipment?' The only police equipment Pel ever trusted was his own brain.

'Computers. That sort of thing.'

Pel sniffed. Computers usually produced only meaningless quantities of statistics of crushing banality such as – as if they didn't know – that eighty-five per cent of the prison population in the Republic was of below normal intelligence.

'I shall manage,' he said.

Rochemare smiled. 'Well, since this is likely to interfere with your holiday – '

'Honeymoon,' Pel snapped. 'And it hasn't started yet.'

Rochemare bowed. He had the look of one of those great lovers from the old films you saw on television. Just a little past his prime. Probably he'd had more than a dozen honeymoons.

'If I may make a suggestion,' he continued, 'since this is likely to interfere with your celebration, then may I offer you, later in the year, at any time of your choosing, another holiday here at my expense. Either at my house or at a house in my grounds which was built originally for my daughter, Elodie. Unfortunately at the moment it's being repaired so it's not available, but it has every convenience – luxury even – and there would be a staff who would administer to your needs, while everything – food, wine, transport – would be at my expense. For the meantime, something more than adequate will be provided at no cost to yourself.'

Pel eyed him warily. It was a generous offer and Pel, being Pel, felt obliged to consider it. In any case, it seemed, he had no option.

'I shall have to speak to my wife,' he said.

Madame Pel was in no doubt about what they should do. 'Since you have no option,' she said, 'then you must accept. After all, a house – doubtless a big house, too – with a staff to do all the work would be excellent. I think we can wait a little longer.'

'And what will you do in the meantime? I'm going to be busy. It's a murder case.'

'I shall be comfortable. The Vicomte promised I should. If not I shall find an apartment myself. In the village, so I shall feel safe. We can afford it.'

Pel said nothing. He was always impressed by the way his new wife threw money about as if there were no tomorrow. On his wedding day he had been surprised to find how many imposing relatives she possessed. Her side of the church had been packed solid with terrifyingly wealthy people while his own had contained only his sister from Chatillon, where her husband ran a men's clothiers, and the sister married to an

Englishman who – highly amused that, after years of dodging, her little brother had finally allowed himself to be caught – had felt she had to make the trip. Apart from these, there were only a few colleagues from the Hôtel de Police. The Chief, of course, the Maire, the Prefect, Judge Polverari, whom Pel liked, and Judge Brisard, whom he detested but had to invite – all very necessary if he were to retain their favour. The rest was made up of people like Detective Sergeants Nosjean, momentarily uninvolved with a girl, De Troquereau, Darel, Lagé and Misset, of his team – though he would gladly have left out Misset who could almost be expected to ruin the show with his stupidity – Inspector Nadauld, of the Uniformed Branch; Inspector Pomereu, of Traffic; Inspector Goriot, the Co-ordinator; Minet, the police doctor; Leguyader, of Forensic; Grenier, of Photography; and Prélat, of Fingerprints; all people whose good will it was important to keep. Finally, there were the newspapermen – who had to be there because a warm relationship with the press – 'Make sure there's plenty of booze for them,' Pel had said – was essential to good policing. Not a very prepossessing lot on the whole. And not a millionaire among them.

'Won't you go home?' he asked.

'And leave you here? Of course not. I shall expect to see you occasionally, surely.'

'You'll be alone a lot of the time.'

'Then I shall telephone my sister Berthe and get her to come and share the place with me. She's unmarried and has money, and she's always complaining she doesn't get enough holiday.'

'You'd do that? To be with me? What about your business?'

'It'll manage without me. I have an excellent staff. If we lose a little custom, we'll soon recover it.'

Pel couldn't imagine what he'd ever done to produce such devotion. Loneliness he could imagine, but losing money! He was deeply touched.

'It's not my idea of a honeymoon,' he said.

She smiled. 'It's not mine either. But you have your job to do. If you do it well, one day you'll probably be Commissaire of Police in Paris.'

The very thought made Pel shudder. He loved the thought of Paris as he loved the thought of Hell. It was too far from

Burgundy and, stuck away in the barbaric north, was very nearly outside France. All the same, it was pleasant to feel that she should think him capable of holding such a position.

'After all,' she went on. 'As I've found in business, you have to take your chances when they come. If you don't, they're gone for ever.'

He saw why she was wealthy.

By the afternoon, they were installed not in an apartment as they'd expected but in a house overlooking the bay in the Vieux Port. It was modern, well-furnished and looked as if it had belonged to someone with money. Pel suspected that Rochemare had turned out at a moment's notice whoever owned it, because there was still food in the cupboards and the place showed signs of having been recently occupied. It was a touch smart and over-coloured, however, and had been decorated with the sort of taste that made Madame, whose taste was impeccable, wince a little. Nevertheless, it had been furnished with an eye to comfort, though there were just too many objets d'art about it, small Dresden figurines, china birds, silver snuff boxes, and so on. One whole table of them that seemed permanently in the way and in danger of being knocked flying gave Pel a fit of nerves just to look at it, so that he wondered who would turn over their house at a moment's notice, complete with all its treasures, for a totally unknown police officer and his wife.

A Peugeot that looked familiar and a small Renault in the garage were also at their disposal, it seemed, and it was only as Pel was inspecting them that he found a pile of brochures advertising villas about the island stamped with the name 'Pierre Dupont' and realised the house had belonged to the smiling treacherous couple who had welcomed them to the Villa des Roses the previous night. For the first time, he warmed towards Rochemare. Justice, it seemed, sometimes prevailed.

By the time he returned to the house, a car was just drawing up. It was one of Rochemare's maids, who had been put at their disposal. She was a young woman in her late twenties by the name of Nelly Biazz, pretty, dark-haired, dark-eyed, intelligent-looking and full of smiles.

'I used to work with the Vicomte's daughter, Elodie,' she

said. 'She was lonely, because the Vicomte was often away on business – he still is – and she liked to talk to me. There was no one else, I suppose, because his wife's also always away in Spain. She never seems to come home.'

The fact that the Vicomte's daughter liked and trusted Nelly reassured them at once. She would do all the work, she said, so that despite the circumstances, Madame's holiday could still be a real one and she would also sleep in, so that Madame would never be alone.

'I know what to do,' she said. She held up her arm and indicated a gold bracelet she wore on her wrist. 'I was given this by someone I looked after as a mark of thanks.'

Meanwhile a telephone call had already gone to Lyons and Madame's sister had agreed to appear in a day or two.

'So – ' considering what they'd just experienced, Madame looked remarkably cheerful ' – you can safely go to your work and we'll look forward to another splendid holiday later in the year at the Vicomte's expense.'

By the time Pel returned to the Villa des Roses, the police had placed tapes all round the grounds. It was impossible to seal it up because the doors wouldn't lock, but Beauregard informed Pel that the Duponts had been ordered to replace the locks as soon as the fingerprint experts had arrived from Nice and gone over the place. Once again, justice seemed to be prevailing.

Caceolari's car, its steering wheel covered with blood and with more blood on the driver's seat, still stood at the top of the slope, guarded like the house by an impassive policeman who looked more Italian than French, and on the scree slope tapes had also been strung round deep scars made by feet in the loose surface of the slope.

'These are the prints made by Caceolari as he ran down,' Beauregard said. 'There are other prints, obviously made by whoever was chasing him. Then there are prints going up again. They're easy to identify because, you'll remember, it rained last night, heavy enough to blur the ones you made when you arrived. There are tyre marks up there as well, and they coincide with Caceolari's tyres. But there are also others which can't be identified. They're smooth like Caceolari's so they never will be, I expect. Everybody has smooth tyres here.'

'Does no one on this island ever replace them?' There was a touch of acid in Pel's voice.

'It isn't necessary, Chief. You can't go very fast anywhere because the roads are too winding and we never get snow.' Beauregard shrugged. 'It looks to me as though someone followed him up here from the village and that he knew he was being followed. He tried to get down the slope but he wasn't quick enough. We found blood on the slope, as if that was where they caught up with him.'

'What was he coming down the slope for?'

Beauregard shrugged. 'To see you, Chief? His wife said he mentioned meeting a famous detective off the ferry.'

Pel frowned. It seemed very likely. Especially in view of Caceolari's obvious anxiety to talk. Perhaps he'd seen something illegal going on and felt he should report it. He couldn't think of any other reason. 'Who is he, this Caceolari?' he asked.

'Paolo Caceolari. Italian background originally. A lot of Italians came here from the Italian mainland in the last century. Political reasons. Sometimes they were wanted by the Italian police. A lot of families here sprang from them.' Beauregard gestured at the policeman standing in the doorway of the house. 'Nizzi's one. His family came originally from Sardinia.'

'What about Caceolari's?'

'Corsica, I think. Before it became French.'

'Could it be some sort of vendetta? They flourish there.'

'They flourish here, Chief. We've had a few knifings in our time. No mystery though. They were soon discovered, because everybody knew everybody else's family feuds.'

'Was Caceolari involved in a feud?'

'Nobody knows of one.'

'Was he *just* a taxi driver?'

'That was what he was supposed to be. But half the time his taxi wouldn't go – puncture, flat battery, no petrol – and one of the farmers or Lesage from the garage would turn out with their own cars. Still, I suppose you'd *say* he was a taxi driver. But he was a bit of an odd-job man too, Chief. Everybody here does several jobs.'

'What a pity the police don't,' Pel said. 'If they did, we could have sorted out the fingerprints by this time. What about the doctor? Who's he?'

'Doctor Nicolas. Local man. Lives near Mortcerf. Alone, except for his cat. Drinks a bit. But people trust him. He's pretty old. You can't get youngsters to come here.'

'Why not?'

'Too far from the mainland. No discotheques, except during the summer season when the holidaymakers want to dance. No big football matches. Only between the villages and they're pretty grim. The pitches are usually at an angle of forty-five degrees because there's nowhere flat on the island. There's also no bingo, and television reception's poor and the kids don't like it because *they're* into video and electronics. So they grow bored and go to the mainland to find work as soon as they're old enough. The clever ones even go as boarders for school. It's the only way they can get into universities and a lot never come back. In a few years time there'll be nobody here but old men and women.'

Pel had heard the story before. It seemed to be common to all offshore islands.

'I shall need an assistant,' he suggested. 'Who's your brightest man?'

Beauregard, who seemed to be a realist, shrugged. 'There aren't any bright ones, Chief.'

'How about you?'

'Chief, I have to run the whole island. There isn't much in the way of crime, but there's a lot of paperwork.'

Pel considered. 'I'd better get one of my team here then,' he said. 'Will the island's finances stand it?'

'The Vicomte's will, Chief.'

Pel paused. 'Who is this Vicomte, anyway?' he asked. 'Old title or one he made up himself? There are a few of those about.'

Beauregard grinned. 'It's a genuine enough, Chief,' he said. 'Second Empire brand. Granted to his great-grandfather about 1862. I think the old boy helped Napoleon III in some financial fiddle or over some dame.'

'And will he pay *all* expenses?'

'Everything, Chief. Anything you want. It's *his* island. Me and my boys, we're sort of really on loan. The French government insists on having its police here, but the Vicomte pays our wages.'

'How many helpers would he stand for?'

'Certainly one. Perhaps two, if you insisted. He's got more money than he knows what to do with. In addition to the big hotel here, the ferries to the mainland and to Calvi in Corsica, and the farms he owns, he has interests in oil, coal, steel, plastic and the import and export business. He's probably one of the wealthiest men in France.'

Pel nodded. 'In that case,' he said. 'I'll need to use your telephone.'

4

By evening, the Chief had agreed to release one of Pel's squad to assist him and Sergeant Charles-Victor De Troquereau could be expected to arrive some time the following day.

Pel had thought a lot about whom to employ. Darcy, of course, was ruled out at once because someone had to go on running the department. So was Nosjean, the senior sergeant, for the same reason. Misset never had a chance. Lazy, careless, bored with his marriage, always with the threat of being returned to the uniformed branch hanging over him, Misset was the last man Pel wanted. Lagé? He was friendly and willing enough but he lacked imagination. Claudie Darel was clever but he needed a man. The rest of the team, Aimedieu, Brochard, Debray and the others were all new boys, not really tested as yet, though Aimedieu seemed to have the makings of a good sleuth. It left only De Troq', and Pel had decided on De Troq' long since, anyway.

Self-confident and keen, De Troq' was the exact opposite of Misset and another in the line of Darcy and Nosjean, never whining about evenings off and always managing to slot his private life into the gaps left by his work. Besides, Pel had a feeling that De Troq' would suit his purpose for another reason. It looked very much as though he would be working closely with the Vicomte de la Rochemare and Pel suspected that out of his whole squad De Troq' was best suited for that task. Educated to the extent of speaking several languages, arrogant, handsome, De Troq' was a baron – an impoverished one, true, but still with a baron's autocratic manner as Misset who had tried to bully him when he had first joined Pel's squad, had swiftly discovered. The Baron Charles-Victor de Troquereau Tournay-Turenne wouldn't let *anyone* push him around and in him the Vicomte de la Rochemare, Pel considered, would surely find his equal. If nothing else De Troq's

34

title belonged to the Old Régime, and that, Pel decided, immediately put him in a higher league altogether than Rochemare.

Because he felt he needed to get the feel of the place, Pel and his wife took their dinner in one of the small restaurants that huddled round the harbour of the Vieux Port. Signs of the approaching holiday season were everywhere. The place stank of fresh paint and at every small hole in a wall that would eventually sport a bar or a disco someone was applying colour. Away from the ferry harbour, however, at that moment there was only one bar open near the sea. Judging by the decorations, it catered chiefly for the locals but clearly its owners were after tourists, too, and tables had been placed on the sea wall alongside. The landlord's wife was putting out the Martini-decorated umbrellas, and the landlord himself was stringing coloured lights over the door.

There was even a newspaper to read. Not a new one, to be sure, but one which had come over on the ferry that afternoon. It was still speculating about the shooting of the six men in the Bar-Tabac de la Porte in Nice and the questioning of the Minister responsible for the Bureau of Environmental Surveys, and it was pleasant to be reminded that there were other places in the world besides the Ile de St. Yves. And when Pel managed to find a paragraph about a nine-car pile-up on the Autoroute du Sud near Avallon in Burgundy he felt almost at home.

The owner of the restaurant, who was also putting the finishing touches to a paint job on the door, stood aside as they arrived and welcomed them with his arms widespread. 'Come in,' he said. 'You're my first customers this season. As you can see, I'm still getting the place ready.'

He took his paintpots through the back door of the restaurant to where they could see a small cobbled yard that contained several stone outhouses, and returned a moment later, wiping his hands on a towel. 'Turidu Riccio, at your service,' he said. 'Turidu's short for Salvatore.'

'Everybody knows Turidu,' Beauregard had said. 'Just ask for Turidu. You'll be all right.'

They had to be. Since the season hadn't yet got going, Turidu Riccio's restaurant was the only one open.

Riccio himself was a tall man with broad shoulders, burly, strong – a fisherman, he admitted, out of the holiday season – with a set of gold teeth that looked as if they had come direct from the vaults of the Banque de France. As they talked, Pel realised he'd been one of the group of men standing in the shelter of the bar in the Vieux Port when they'd landed, leaning on a wall beneath the sign *Save food. Eat tourists* – the group of men who'd pushed Caceolari's car when it had refused to start.

'I've seen you before,' he said.

'Of course, Monsieur.' Riccio dazzled him with his gold teeth in a wide smile. 'Everybody knows me.'

'You were standing outside one of the bars yesterday. One near the ferry jetty.'

'I am always near the jetty when the ferry arrives.'

'Why?'

Riccio placed one finger against his nose. 'It's an island pastime, Monsieur. To study the girls who come to spend their holidays here. To look them over and study the form. I'm not married, so why not? Everybody else does. You'd be surprised what goes on during the summer season.'

Pel had heard of the behaviour of girls from the north – from England, Germany, Holland, Belgium and the Scandinavian countries. The Mediterranean sun seemed to make harlots of them at once and the first thing they did was involve themselves in a torrid affair with a local man – be he barman, waiter or chef – which sometimes left them a month or two later with grave worries about their future.

'He seemed nervous of you,' Pel said.

Riccio shrugged. 'He owed me money and I am big.'

'Had you threatened him or something?'

'Caceolari? Me?' Riccio laughed. 'I didn't have to. He knew he had to pay.'

'What would have happened if he hadn't?'

'Probably a punch on the jaw, Monsieur.'

'Not a knife in the chest?'

Riccio laughed. 'They told me you were a cop, Monsieur. I think you're thinking like a cop.'

Yes, Pel thought. He was. He'd have to try to stop. Tonight at least. After all, despite everything, he *was* on his honeymoon.

36

'Caceolari was a nervous type, Monsieur,' Riccio went on. 'These Italian types get nervous very quickly. You can tell by the name he was Italian.'

'Yours is Riccio. That sounds Italian, too. Where did your family come from?'

'Sicily,' Riccio grinned. 'We're a bit tougher in Sicily.'

Pel's questions didn't seem to worry him and he continued the business of settling them in with a large smile and considerable flair.

'What'll it be for an apéritif?' he asked.

They decided on a dry vermouth so Riccio placed the bottle on the table with a slam. 'Help yourselves,' he said cheerfully.

There was a fine dry local wine and expertly cooked swordfish steaks. The fact that Riccio handled the fish with the same hand he used to put more charcoal on the grill hardly mattered at all and Pel had one glass of wine too many, so that he ended up more mellow under the circumstances than he'd expected, and even complimented Riccio on the meal.

'I catch the fish I serve myself,' Riccio said. 'That's my boat.' He gestured at the line of vessels tied up to the quay just outside. 'The yellow one.'

'The swordfish was yesterday's fish?'

'Ah, no, Monsieur!' Riccio smiled apologetically. 'Not the swordfish. The mullet and other things. Besides, I've just finished fishing. A week ago.'

'Good catch?'

'Excellent. But today the holiday season starts and the tourists come, so I make more money from my restaurant. And anyway, I don't have the equipment for catching swordfish. That's frozen. But good, no?'

Well, yes, it *was* good, but frozen fish to a man who set such store by his food as Pel did, it wasn't quite the same.

The rain that had been hanging about ever since their arrival seemed finally to have gone and the night was warm, so Pel and his wife went outside to drink their coffee and brandy. It was a new experience for Pel to drink with a woman. Usually his drinking companion was Darcy with his cynical comments on life. As modern as the space age, Darcy knew exactly what life was all about and his attitude to women and to his work were brisk and realistic. This was different. Pel felt like holding his breath as he looked at Madame. How he had induced her to marry *him* he couldn't imagine, and he still lived in fear that even now she might abandon him for someone more handsome, clever and rich. Perhaps it was the light or perhaps it was just the fact that she was on her honeymoon, but at that moment she looked beautiful in a way he'd never noticed before. It made him ashamed of his growing baldness and uninspiring frame. It was his firm view that he resembled a rather bad-tempered terrier and that what was left of his hair lay across his head like wet streaks on a rainy pavement. For the life of him, he couldn't work out how he'd managed to win her. At an age when he'd begun to suspect life had shot by him and he was condemned to old age with only Madame Routy, his housekeeper, to keep him company, an old age, moreover, which – despite the fact that he'd been stuffing savings away for years – would, in addition, also be poverty-stricken, he had acquired a wife who was not only good to look at but also possessed wealth beyond his dreams.

With his house already let, they had acquired a new house and Madame was now converting into an apartment rooms over her business premises so that Pel wouldn't have to trail home from the city when emergencies kept him late at the office. Finally, she was also exploring the possibility of buying a weekend house on a lake in the Jura. Suddenly Pel had become a bloated plutocrat.

As they waited for their coffee, Riccio moved about, serving other customers who had appeared, then he banged down on their table a miniature Espresso-type machine and plugged it into the socket where the table light was connected.

'Help yourself,' he said cheerfully. 'I am busy.'

Madame was intrigued. The machine was not a lot taller than a normal percolater, but was bright red, with a wide central column on a square stand that held cups and saucers. The column supported a small square tank which, when she peeped inside, was found to contain water.

'That's useful for a home,' she observed.

'I can get you one,' Riccio said. 'They're assembled here on the island so we get them cheap. Soon they'll come in different colours. There's enough water in there for half a dozen cups. All you have to do is put in the coffee and press the switch. It heats the water and pours it through the coffee into the cup. I have several. They're cheaper than hiring help – especially when I'm busy. And I sometimes am in the summer when the tourists come.'

As they sat in the warm evening, silence descended on them. Pel was entranced. Despite the happenings of the day, his marriage filled him with so much pleasure and amazement he wished he could purr. If nothing else, it had relieved him for ever of the ill-temper of Madame Routy, his housekeeper. For years Madame Routy had bullied him with half-cooked casseroles for the simple reason that, being addicted to the box with the square eye in the salon, she could never tear herself away long enough to give her full attention to the stove. He had been terrified when the new Madame Pel had insisted on taking her over with Pel but, since Madame ran a hairdressing salon which was noted not only for the ability of its operators to persuade wealthy women to submit them-selves to the torments caused by ever-changing hairstyles but also for its ability to charge them vast sums of money for the privilege, he had finally though somewhat unwillingly agreed. And, on the very first occasion when Madame Routy had tried her hand at a meal for them, she had surprised him with what she had produced. He could only suppose that his wife had more skill at dealing with female staff than he had. He wondered if, under the circumstances, he ought to risk another cigarette but summoning up his reserves – and it needed a few – he decided against it.

'No,' he said with the air of an early Christian martyr about to face the lions. 'No cigarettes after the one I have with my evening meal.'

'When did you decide that?'

'Just now.'

Madame gave him a doubtful smile. 'Think you can keep it up?'

'No,' he admitted.

They walked back to the house along the harbour hand in hand, Pel feeling faintly like a bashful boy but defiant about it nevertheless. As they entered the Duponts' splendid house and closed the door, Madame turned to smile at him. 'I hope nobody drops dead on us tonight,' she said.

5

The first visitor to the Duponts' house was the postman who brought letters and catalogues for the Duponts.

'They'll collect them eventually,' he said, tossing them into the garage.

He was a cheerful young man with a long face, glasses and a mandarin moustache. Inevitably he didn't wear a postman's grey suit but jeans, a red T-shirt with UNIVERSITY OF CALIFORNIA stamped across it and the usual canvas shoes.

'They've got a good business here,' he said. 'How come they rented you their own house? I've never known them do anything like that before.'

Pel was standing on the verandah while Madame bathed and dressed and, because it was a bright morning, warm and sunny with no sign of rain clouds, he was willing to listen to the postman's gossip. Gossip, his shrewd policeman's instinct told him, sometimes contained a lot of truths.

'They didn't rent it,' he said. 'They – ah – lent it to us. I think they were encouraged by the Vicomte de la Rochemare.'

The postman gave him a sharp look. 'You that cop that's come to the island to sort out this Caceolari thing?'

'I am that cop,' Pel said stiffly. 'But I didn't come here for that reason. I came for a holiday.'

'Well, apart from the big stuff and the millionaires' set-ups at Muriel on the other side of the island, you've got one of the best houses there are. No swimming pool, mind, but *I* wouldn't mind having it, I can tell you. Me and my wife still have to share with her mother. What's more, here in the Vieux Port it's not likely to catch fire.'

Pel remembered what he'd been told as he arrived on the ferry. 'I hear houses have a habit of catching fire here,' he said.

'Some do. Only holiday homes though. There's a type

40

going round the island burning them down while their owners are away. A litre or two of paraffin and a match. Paf! It's easy. We call him Guillaume le Feu – Billy the Burner. It suits him, don't you think?'

Pel offered him a glass of white wine. It was a habit of his with postmen and this one seemed to know exactly what went on across the island. As they sat on the verandah, the young man introduced himself.

'Jean Babin,' he said.

'Have you always worked here?' Pel asked.

'Since I left school.'

'Always as a postman?'

'About six years. I sometimes do a few jobs for Lesage at the garage. I'm good with engines. Everybody does two jobs here and being postman's a cushy job. You just collect the mail when it comes off the afternoon ferry then next day you drive it round the island in the van to where it's supposed to go.'

'Tell me more about these houses that are being burned.'

'Well, this type, Billy the Burner, whoever he is, obviously keeps his eyes open, and when he sees a cottage belonging to somebody who isn't an islander empty for a long time, he puts a match to it.'

'Why does he do that?'

Babin laughed. 'Resentment. Objects to people coming to the island. They take over old houses, modernise them, build a swimming pool, then only live in them for two months of the year. A lot of the islanders feel the same.'

'Did you know Caceolari?'

'Not much. Not my type.'

'You get about. Ever see him about the island?'

The postman grinned. 'Often. Always under that car of his. You wouldn't believe the number of times I've been asked to give him a shove to start him or a lift to Lesage's to collect petrol or borrow a battery or a new tyre or something.'

'Ever see him with any strangers?'

'There aren't any strangers on the island.'

'Anybody unusual?'

The postman grinned. 'We're *all* unusual here,' he said, finishing his wine. 'We wouldn't be here, otherwise. I reckon we're all nuts just to stay.'

*
41

Nelly Biazz, the maid sent down by the Vicomte de la Roche-mare to look after them, was preparing breakfast and when Madame announced that she intended to sit in the sunshine with her and find out where the shops were, Pel decided he might as well go to see Beauregard.

'I shall be all right,' Madame said. 'Nelly knows the way and we can both drive. And, of course, there's the little Renault.' She gave Pel a bright smile. 'I suspect the Duponts are having to pay for their shiftiness by renting one of their own hire cars. Probably that old Diane that came on the ferry.'

Driving along the harbour road to the police station in the Duponts' substantial Peugeot, Pel felt like a financial magnate, and to his delight, he spotted the car's owners just ahead of him walking towards their office. As he beamed at them, they gave him a glare of pure hatred that made his day.

The police station was in the main square, alongside a small set of administrative offices, but since the island was administered not by a mayor but by the Vicomte de la Roche-mare, there was no Mairie. The interior was blank and ugly and remarkably dusty.

'It's always dusty,' Beauregard said gloomily. 'When the mistral blows it whips up everything that's been left around.'

Pel wasn't very interested in the climatic problems of the island and got to grips with the real business at once. 'What's the crime rate like here?' he asked.

Beauregard shrugged and scratched his chin. 'There isn't any crime.'

'There is now,' Pel rapped in a voice like the slam of a door. 'Murder.'

Beauregard shrugged again. 'Well, that's unusual, of course. Normally nothing *ever* happens here. Well, not quite nothing. There's been some type going around setting fire to houses. A couple of litres of paraffin and a match when the owner's away.'

'So I've heard. You call that nothing?'

'Well, it's almost nothing. They're all holiday homes belonging to people from the mainland.'

'It's still arson.'

'What I mean,' Beauregard said patiently, 'is that it's

42

nothing to the people who live here. You know what it's like. People from the cities buy cottages and small houses – big ones too – and stick in a swimming pool and a few bougain-villea and geraniums, live in them a few weeks a year, and let them for another few weeks to make them pay. The rest of the year they're empty. There are kids without houses who resent it.'

Pel could see the point. It was all part of the scene that had sprung from high-speed travel and it was occurring in every country in the world. Jaded city dwellers anxious for a country retreat were buying up all sorts of old cottages and farms and converting them into modernised living quarters and then recouping their cost by letting them during the summer season. It not only changed the face of the country-side but it was also not much help to young people wanting to marry and set up home in the village where they were born, grew up and wanted to go on living. Even as he sympa-thised, he was guiltily aware that he and his new wife were thinking of doing the same thing in the Jura so he could have the pleasure of a little weekend fishing.

'What are you doing about it?' he asked.

Beauregard shrugged. 'Isn't much you *can* do,' he said. 'I make a few enquiries but nobody ever knows anything. People keep a tight lip. *In bocca chiusa non entra mai mosca.*'

'What's that?'

'It's an old Italian saying. The people on the island use it.'

'What's it mean?'

'A fly never enters a closed mouth. They don't talk much.'

It was something Pel had come across before. In some of the higher regions of France, the people seemed to prefer to maintain their isolation and went weeks without speaking to anyone else. There were occasionally even hatreds and fierce passions and few ideas on anything else and, though the people were not educated they were crafty with the wisdom of experience and sometimes wealthy far beyond their outward appearance.

Doubtless Beauregard didn't push the matter of the burnings too hard. The arrest of an islander for an offence of which the islanders approved might have made his position there very uncomfortable.

He was still brooding on the matter when Beauregard

announced that he'd arranged for Pel to see the Vicomte again. Pel looked up sharply, feeling he was being managed.

'Why are we going to see the Vicomte?' he asked.

'I thought you'd like to. He's invited you to lunch.'

Pel had felt that he could conduct his enquiries in his own way with access to the Vicomte only when things grew difficult and he needed his authority to sort them out. Nevertheless, they were collected by the Vicomte's Range Rover, a vast British machine like a tank that was polished to the point of being dazzling.

'He lives in style,' Pel said.

'Oh, this isn't his normal car,' Beauregard assured him. 'He uses a big Citroën. This is just for other people.'

Such as visiting chief inspectors, Pel thought sourly, who didn't merit the same treatment as the titled and wealthy the Vicomte normally entertained.

To his surprise, the Vicomte's château, though not an old one, had been built as a replica of one of the châteaux of the Loire. It was small, of white local stone, and was built in front of a wide circular tree-shaded lake – artifically made, he felt sure – on which there were swans. Beyond the lake were hectares of parkland and a view of the sun on the sea. They drove in through huge wrought-iron gates and circled the building by a wide turreted tower, which Beauregard said contained the library. Beyond the front door there was a huge hall leading into a long corridor that ran the length of the building.

'My son,' Beauregard murmured, 'thought it would be a good place to set up his model railway.'

Pel gave his smile time to settle before he replied. 'It's in good condition,' he admitted.

'It's one of the few châteaux that's fully used and lived in. It's not too big and it pays for its own upkeep. He converted the stables into freezers and people come here every day to prepare vegetables grown on the island ready to go into them. He was one of the first to get into it when France started eating frozen foods.'

Pel said nothing. It had long been his opinion that frozen, packaged and preserved foods had ruined French culinary expertise. Doubtless Madame Routy, who had given him indigestion for years, had learned to cook with frozen food and it was well known that people were nowadays so stuffed with preservatives from the food they ate, there was no need to embalm them when they died.

They were shown into the library. On a table was a visitors' book. Beauregard looked over Pel's shoulder and opened it. 'See that?' he said. 'Notice the names? Teddy Roosevelt. Edward VII. Queen Marie of Rumania. Alexander of Jugoslavia. Winston Churchill. Onassis. Callas. I bet he won't ask *us* to sign it. Like his father before him, he's had his good times here, believe me. Women, for instance. He had quite a reputation. Still has, come to that.'

The Vicomte arrived soon afterwards, followed by a manservant with drinks. He looked more than ever like a broken-down roué.

'Your wife, Monsieur?' he said to Pel. 'You didn't bring her?'

'I left her talking to the maid you sent down. They seemed to be getting on very well together.'

'Next time you *must* bring her.'

'I suspect I may be too busy to make social calls.'

'Then I'll look after her. We might have dinner together. You must send her up on her own.'

Not on your life, Pel thought. I wouldn't trust you, mon brave, with anything under ninety. Perhaps not even that.

They were joined by a large broad-shouldered Italian-looking man called Tissandi, who turned out to be the Vicomte's agent and handled all his business on the island, his freezer plants, his imports and exports, the boutiques and hotels he owned. Like the Vicomte, he was immaculately dressed in casual clothes which, Pel decided, must have cost a bomb, but were finished off as usual with the usual canvas-topped rope-soled shoes.

'I live here in the château,' he pointed out. 'I have an office and an apartment at the back with my own entrance. I also have an office in the Vieux Port. If there's anything you need just call in there. If I'm not there the clerk will put you through by telephone to my office here, and I can always send the car for you. Anyone will direct you, just ask for the Ufficio. It's the old Italian name for it. The island was originally Italian. The Italians used to claim Nice and Corsica, of course, and a lot of people here have Italian backgrounds. I'm one.'

'With twenty years of devotion to me,' the Vicomte said. 'He does all my worrying, all my dirty work, all my hard labour, so I can carry on with my decadent and slothful way of life, knowing perfectly well that my property, my estate, my business interests, my finances are in safe hands.'

'For which,' Tissandi pointed out, 'I'm very well repaid. When I first came here I was just a small boy with an Italian background and little education. You fitted me for the job.'

'Doing what?' It seemed to Pel to be about time to interrupt the duologue of mutual admiration with some blunt facts. 'Exactly?'

Tissandi turned. 'We're involved in many things. Olive oil. Imports into the island. Aluminium-tube folding chairs. Tubular garden furniture. It comes from Italy – '

'Coffee machines?'

'You've seen them?' Tissandi laughed. 'They come on the St. Yves-Calvi ferry. There are other things too. Sulphur, for instance. It comes from the west side of the island, in a barren area known as L'Aride. It's found in its free state in many volcanic districts like Sicily. This island was originally a volcano. To free it from impurities we stack it in brick kilns and ignite it with burning brushwood. The heat causes it to melt and flow into moulds and it's then sent away by ship for purification.' He gestured. 'It's obtained in other ways, of course, but this is the old simple method. It's used for many things – metallurgy, chemicals, cements, petrol refining, medicaments, insecticides, fungicides, fertilisers. There are two natural reserves here and as an insurance against a possible shortage, the government pays us subsidies to store it, not sell it. It's a new government policy. It's been operating for some time now. They're considering the possibility of some national emergency – war, disaster, strikes, something of that sort, even sabotage – and the likelihood of industry running short. It's happening with most other countries in the Western bloc and with other producers both in France and abroad. Decided at Foreign Minister level, I believe. It's my job to handle the business involved.'

The meal was served on flattish metal plates of a pale yellow colour. Pel couldn't take his eyes off them. Tissandi

46

saw the way he was studying his meal and, as the Vicomte was called to the telephone, he leaned over and whispered.

'Your suspicions do you credit, Chief,' he murmured. 'They *are* gold. The Vicomte likes to impress people sometimes. It seems he wanted to impress you.'

What with, Pel wondered. His power? His wealth? Or the fact that he held the island in the palm of his hand?

Beauregard had noticeably disappeared and Pel suspected he was being given *his* meal in the kitchen – if he were being given one at all.

There were several menservants to serve them, something which irritated Pel. If you couldn't manage to eat a meal without half a dozen people waiting to hand you things, you had to be either damned lazy or suffering from a stroke. Several times he pushed away the white-gloved hands that reached forward to pass him a spoon.

'Of course, I help run the estate, too,' the Vicomte explained. 'My father, the Duc de Dudecheville, who owns it, is gaga, you see. I think my wife is a little gaga, too. She spends all her time and all my money trying to provide baths for the caves of the gypsies in Spain.'

By this time Pel was beginning to wonder if they were ever going to get down to business. Caceolari was lying on a cold slab somewhere – in one of the Vicomte's freezers, he'd been told, because there was no mortuary nearer than Nice where he could be kept – and the trail, if there were a trail, was cooling rapidly.

They took coffee on the terrasse where they were joined by a tall dark languid man in the same expensive casual dress and canvas shoes. He looked so wilting he seemed on the point of collapse.

'My secretary,' the Vicomte introduced. 'Freddy Ignazi. He also lives in the château.'

Ignazi held out a limp hand to be shaken and managed a weak smile as he folded up into a cane chair. He was in the same mould as the Vicomte – thin body, thin arms and legs, and thin neck – but somehow while the Vicomte was whipcord, Ignazi was just strengthless pith.

'*Baron* Ignazi,' Tissandi whispered. 'The Vicomte likes to be surrounded by titles.'

When they finally got down to business, Pel noticed that

Beauregard had reappeared, an overweight, undershaved man with sly eyes. He looked satisfied with himself so Pel assumed he'd been adequately fed and watered. He hadn't seen him arrive, had suddenly merely noticed him sitting in one of the cane chairs, stiffly upright as if he were on parade and on his best behaviour, trying hard to manipulate a minute cup and saucer with his huge hairy hands. He could only assume that when the coffee had been ordered, instructions had gone to the kitchen for him to put in an appearance.

'This is the first major crime we've had on the island in years,' the Vicomte said. 'Of course there are these burnings of holiday homes, though I have a certain sympathy with whoever's doing it.'

'It's against the law, whoever's doing it,' Pel said stiffly.

The Vicomte sighed. 'Of course. But my sympathy tends to lie with the young people. I'd like to keep them here and there are *some* who'd prefer to be here, in a house with a garden where they can grow things, keep chickens and see the sea.' He gestured. 'I've built a few houses to let, of course, and even helped a few youngsters with loans, especially if their parents or they themselves work for me. To be quite honest, it doesn't worry me if we never catch our arsonist. It might discourage people from the mainland from buying our houses.'

When they finally got around to Caceolari, Rochemare was quick to understand the way Pel was thinking and was wondering what it was that Caceolari had been afraid of.

'He was afraid of *something* and it led to his death,' Pel said. 'I think he'd have liked to have told me.'

Rochemare looked up. 'Did he?'

'No. He changed his mind.' Pel paused. 'Who were his friends? Whom did he know?'

Rochemare looked at Beauregard who shrugged.

'Everybody,' Beauregard said. 'Nobody in particular. He was the taxi-driver. The only one on the island. Everybody knew him.'

'Was he involved in anything?'

Beauregard shrugged.

'Politics?'

Another shrug.

48

'The Mafia?' Rochemare asked. 'The Marseilles gangs? After all, we're not far from either Marseilles or Italy.'

Another shrug.

'Then something must have sparked it off while I was on my way here,' Pel said. 'What was it?'

Rochemare and Beauregard studied each other. 'Nothing ever happens here,' Rochemare said. 'Except that Fleurie, the storekeeper behind the harbour of the Vieux Port, ran off with Pinchon's wife. Madame Fleurie runs a foreign exchange on the island. She's known as the Black Widow. She isn't a widow but she's always looked like one. It's no wonder Fleurie ran off with Madame Pinchon. I heard they were in Toulouse.'

'He was always telephoning her to meet him,' Beauregard said.

'How do you know?' Pel asked.

Beauregard grinned. 'Everybody knows everything on this island. Most of the telephones are party lines. You know how they work. Six people on the same line. One ring for the first, two for the second and so on. Easiest thing in the world to listen in to someone else's conversation so long as you don't have a coughing fit. It used to be a favourite pastime listening in to Fleurie and Madame Pinchon.'

'There can't be many secrets.'

'There aren't. Mademoiselle Misard, who runs the exchange, always listens in anyway. It's still hand-operated and she has to get you your number. She's been doing it for years.'

'Is that the limit of what goes on?'

They all looked at each other and shrugged.

'What about the mainland? Nice has it's problems and it's not very far away. And I know there's been trouble between the groups operating rival casinos. People have disappeared suddenly. Events there could have their effect here.'

Rochemare's shoulders moved. 'I thought statistics showed that serious crime there was diminishing.'

'It doesn't alter the fact that they still *have* crime,' Pel said. 'Every city has crime. The way a dog has fleas. The casinos were even shut down. And there was that big shooting there last week. Six men mown down in a bar. It's out of my parish, but I'll want to know about it. A thing like that could send ripples out to a lot of strange places. Could Caceolari have been involved?'

Tissandi leaned forward. 'He went to the mainland from time to time,' he said.

'Could he have picked something up? Heard something? Something he shouldn't have?'

Nobody could suggest anything so Pel tried from another angle.

'Where was he just before he arrived in my courtyard?' he asked. 'He obviously wasn't at home with his wife. Did he have a girl friend?'

Rochemare smiled. 'There's that woman at Mortcerf. That's a village in the hills. Name of Robles. Luz Robles. Claims to be Spanish. Supposed to be the ex-madame of a Marseilles brothel. She runs a bar. It's called "La Nida de la Paloma". It means "The Dove's Nest". I heard he sometimes went there at night after she closed.'

'What time *does* she close?'

'In summer, when the holidaymakers are here, after midnight. At this time of the year, around ten. If she bothers to open at all.'

'I think we'd better go and see her as soon as we've seen his widow.'

'Might be a good idea to go and see her *first*,' Beauregard suggested. 'His widow's in no state to see anyone at the moment.'

6

The Ile de St. Yves was a strange place. The Vieux Port was in a flat basin of fertile land called by its old Italian name, the Conca d'Argento, the Silver Shell, and around it the sea showed through the trees in an ever-changing pattern of blue, purple and green, while the hills behind cut into the azure sky like pointed teeth.

The lower slopes were fringed with a straggly covering of cactus – chiefly the prickly pear and the spiky sisal that grew so abundantly further south in places like Riccio's Sicily, each tapering leaf ending in a long black spike hard as ebony and sharp as a needle. Passing carts and occasional cars stirred up a white dust that left all foliage by the roadside greyish and dead-looking, and the land itself looked as dry as a desert.

Dark valleys were obscured by big sweeps of strong colour, the deep ultramarine of the sea, and the pale grey-green of the surrounding olives. Here and there were patches of wheat but, despite the cultivation, there seemed little sign of habitation beyond an occasional herd of cattle or a few goats or sheep. There were no small birds and no bird song and it was a harsh unfriendly terrain with no wild life apart from green and black adders, lizards, large spiders, and a few big bright butterflies, a hybrid sort of place that belonged further south yet somehow seemed to flourish just off the southern coast of France.

Though he was in the affair now too deeply to back out, Pel had no liking for it because the island was like some of the highland villages in mainland France where he'd had to conduct enquiries on other occasions. Away from the harbours and beaches frequented by the tourists, there was no sound, just an incredible silence in the sunshine; and among the hills, with their rocky slopes and crowding trees, the village streets were empty. Even the chickens moved as little as possible in the open because of the hawks that circled the sky. The everlasting wind corroded the landscape and lifted the dust in whorls, and there seemed to be no such thing as an island community. In some of the villages the houses had long been empty and the isolated farms saw no visitors with the exception of Caceolari and perhaps the postman, as they went about their business.

The road from the Vieux Port lifted sharply round the slopes between tall pines and past the little stony track that led to the Villa des Roses. As it lifted higher, the pines gave way to olive groves, the trees twisted into unimaginable shapes like hobgoblins among the rocks.

Mortcerf was a mere huddle of houses all built of the same grey stone as the rest of the island but not plastered and painted white like the houses where the tourists congregated. 'The Dove's Nest' was a simple bar without any sign, but with a small vine-covered terrasse containing a few tables and chairs. The interior was dark and practically bare of furniture, the high counter taking up most of the room.

Luz Robles was a full-busted woman with what had once been a good figure but was now in middle age running to fat. She wore a bright red skirt and yellow blouse which showed every contour of her full breasts. Round her shoulders she wore a purple scarf and the colours clashed abominably but somehow, with her swarthy complexion, the brilliant black eyes on which she had plastered mascara like a barrier and the thick dark hair only just touched with grey, she was able to get away with them. She looked Spanish all right and only needed a comb and a mantilla to complete the picture.

'Hé, Alois,' she said as Beauregard climbed from the little van he drove.

He nodded warily, so that Pel wondered if he, too, were in the habit of visiting her after hours. Come to that, did Rochemare himself? Despite the colours, it was easy to see that Madame Robles' clothes were good and didn't come from one of the indifferent little boutiques of the Vieux Port that intrigued Madame Pel. They looked fashionable as if they came from Nice, or even Paris.

Beauregard was introducing him. 'This,' he said, 'is Chief Inspector Pel. He's from the mainland. You'll have heard about Paolo.'

The smile faded, 'I heard,' she said.

Beauregard shrugged. 'We'd like to ask you a few questions.'

'Why not his wife?'

'Come on, Luz.' Beauregard's voice grew harsher. 'We all knew about you and him.'

Her eyes hardened. 'A lot of people did a lot of talking,' she said. 'But they knew nothing. He had a shrew of a wife and he came here for company. I gave it to him. And that's all. Company. Nothing more.'

'Was he here the night he was killed?' Pel asked.

'No.'

'You'd better tell the truth, Madame. I can soon find out.' Pel gestured at the other houses of the little hamlet. '*They'll* know. People on this island seem to know everything.'

She said nothing for a moment, then she indicated one of the tables. 'Sit down.'

She disappeared into the bar and returned with glasses and a bottle of white wine. 'Local,' she said to Pel. 'It won't be what you're used to.'

She sloshed the wine into the glasses and stood with one elbow on the bar counter like a Paris prostitute waiting for a customer. *Boire sur le zinc* was definitely her style. As she refilled his glass, Pel found himself staring straight down the front of her blouse. The cleavage was like the Grand Canyon and, to a newly-married man, disturbing.

'Well?' Beauregard asked.

'Yes.' She nodded. 'He was here. For an hour or so. No more.'

'Why didn't you say so at first?'

The dark eyes blazed. 'Because it was nobody's business but his – and mine.'

'It is now,' Pel rapped. 'He's been murdered! Why did he come?'

'To see me. That's all.'

'How was he?'

'Same as always. Complaining about his wife.'

'What did you talk about?'

'All sorts of things. His wife chiefly.'

'What time did he leave?'

'Before midnight. I don't know exactly.'

53

'Where was he going?'

'Home.'

'Did he come often?'

'He didn't live here.'

'But he came regularly?'

'Perhaps once a week. About that.'

'Can you remember the last time? Before the night he was killed.'

'Yes. It was my birthday. He brought me some flowers. Wild flowers. It was a funny little gesture but it was well meant. They were already wilting and I threw them away the next morning. He left about midnight.'

'What day was this?'

'My birthday was the 12th. It was the day after. He was a bit late.'

'And he didn't come again until the night he was killed?'

'No.'

'Forgive me asking this question, Madame,' Pel said. 'But it has to be asked. What was your relationship with him?'

She seemed unperturbed. 'We were friends. What else would we be?'

There were a lot of things they could be. Lovers. Partners in crime.

'For your information,' she said, 'I'm retired. And in any case I didn't go in for that sort of thing. Not even when I was in business. I arranged for other people to do it.'

Pel paused. 'He got around the island a lot,' he said. 'Inevitably. He was a taxi-driver. Did he ever go any further? The mainland, for instance? Italy? Ferries run from here to Nice and from here to Calvi in Corsica.'

Beauregard answered the question. 'Sometimes he went to the mainland.'

Madame Robles shrugged. 'For spare parts for that old rattletrap he ran. Not for much else.'

'He went around twice a month,' Beauregard pointed out. 'Surely he didn't need all that many spare parts.'

Beauregard gestured. 'He did errands for people about the island. Rochemare used him when he wanted things and there was nobody else. He ordered them by telephone and if they couldn't be sent Caceolari went to fetch them. I got him to

54

bring things for me. So did Fleurie. Or at least he did before he ran off with the Pinchon woman.'

'Did he ever go to Corsica?'

'Not that I know of. But he might have. The Vicomte imports a few things from there. He might have gone to pick up something for him.'

'Did he talk about any of these places the night he brought you flowers?'

Madame Robles shook her head. 'Not really. A little bit about those murders in Nice. The radio was going on about them. Just generally most of the time, though.'

'And what about the last time? The night he was killed. What did you talk about that night? Apart from his wife?'

Madame Robles paused. 'Nothing much. He seemed a bit worried.'

'What about?'

She hesitated. 'He didn't say.'

It seemed to Pel that she wasn't telling him all the truth and he would need to see her again. Perhaps without Beauregard, because he'd already decided that Beauregard was probably receiving hand-outs and wasn't told things in case he passed the information on to the people who gave him his hand-outs.

Madame Robles was frowning. 'He said he'd been to see someone,' she volunteered.

'About this thing he was worried about?'

'That's what I thought.'

'But he didn't say what it was? He gave no hint?'

'No. He could be pretty close-mouthed when he wanted to. He saw a lot that he shouldn't. He went all over the island and was always coming on things.'

'What sort of things?'

'Well, he knew about Fleurie and the Pinchon woman before anyone else. I knew that. He'd seen them together more than once.'

'But he gave you no idea what it was this time?'

'No. He just said something about going to see someone.'

'Who was it?'

'He didn't say.'

'A lawyer?'

'He certainly didn't come and see me,' Beauregard said.

Madame Robles shrugged. 'I got on all right with him,'

55

she said. 'He made me laugh. But I didn't know anything about his private life.'

'Did you ever go with him on his trips to the mainland?'

'To Nice?' She laughed. 'With Caceolari? You have to be joking. He was a nice little man I was always pleased to see, but I wouldn't go to Nice with somebody who dressed as he did. Blue suit. Hat that looked as if it were made of wood. White shirt. Black tie. No thank you. When I go to Nice, I go to enjoy myself. I have friends there.'

What sort of friends, Pel wondered. 'What about his wife?' he asked. 'Do you know her?'

'I've met her. She didn't impress me much. It's no wonder he liked to come up here.'

'Did he *often* give you the impression that he was worried?'

'Not often. Sometimes. Chiefly when he was short of money. But everybody's worried about that these days, aren't they? There's not enough of it about. Tourists are in short supply. Prices have shot up.'

And, Pel thought, the Russians are about to roll up the map of Europe and scatter atom bombs like confetti over the whole of creation. It was a gloomy prospect to a man newly entered into the state of wedded bliss.

7

De Troquereau arrived that evening. A room had already been unobtrusively booked for him in one of the smaller hotels.

To Pel's surprise, Nice Police flew him over in a helicopter, which at least showed they were carrying out their end of the bargain, and he arrived full of energy and looking as bright as a stockbroker anticipating a profitable day. His handsome intelligent head turned to study the island, small, neat, his hair crisp and neatly cut. Though he claimed to be the impoverished son of an Auvergnat nobleman, he never seemed to be without money. Perhaps poverty was a relative thing, because his hair was always well-trimmed, his clothes were good and he normally drove a vast car with headlamps like lighthouses, enormous wheels and a flat old-fashioned bonnet secured by a strap. It looked as if it had once raced at Le Mans and probably had.

'How're things?' Pel asked.

De Troq' shrugged. 'Same as always. Fighting crime. Darcy pulled in that type we thought was involved in the bank hold-up at Avallon. He was. He burst into tears and admitted it. Misset fell down on an arrest. And Nosjean's in love again.'

Pel smiled at De Troq's cool summing up. He liked to use De Troq' at times to intimidate people. His car was enough to shake all but the most innocent and his title made people think Pel was head of the Sûreté from Paris. As an accompanying choreography, when he was addressed by Pel, De Troq' had developed a small heel-clicking routine that made people think Pel was personal adviser on state secrets to the President of the Republic.

He had brought newspapers from Nice but, apart from the usual lechery, fraud and mayhem at home and the political fiddling and butchery abroad, they contained little of interest.

As Pel had expected, the Ile de St. Yves was so unimportant to the rest of France that the murder of a simple taxi-driver there hadn't roused the slightest interest on the mainland where the press was still busy solving to their own satisfaction the murders in the Bar-Tabac de la Porte.

Taking him back to the Duponts' house, where Nelly took one look at his handsome features and immediately showed unmistakeable signs of interest, they collected Madame and headed for Riccio's restaurant in the belief that there what they had to say wouldn't be overheard. Immediately they discovered some of the problems of living on a small island before the holiday season had got going. The menu was exactly the same as the previous evening.

'No lobster?' Pel asked.

'No, Monsieur.' Riccio was apologetic.

'No mullet?'

Riccio shrugged sadly and they settled for swordfish again. After all it had been good, though Pel didn't fancy eating it for the rest of his stay. 'It might be a good idea to find somewhere else tomorrow,' he murmured.

'We have a car at our disposal,' Madame said quietly. 'Two cars, in fact. The Duponts' cars. Yesterday I saw them driving that old Diane.'

Pel capped it. '*I* saw them walking,' he said.

Though they ate much the same as they'd eaten the day before, even to charcoal on the fish, De Troq' – who, despite his slight frame, had the appetite of a weight-lifter – never seemed to stop. Since all expenses were on the Vicomte de la Rochemare, it seemed, he said, a pity not to take advantage of it, and he appeared to be stoking up while it was free, for the next three years. Madame watched him fascinated.

As they ate, Pel explained what had happened and, to his surprise, Madame took all the horror out of it by describing as if it were a huge joke the Villa des Roses, the problems of fastening the doors, and the difficulties of taking a bath.

De Troq' had had a few difficulties of his own. 'Nice headquarters had to be pushed a bit,' he said. 'They were in a bit of a state. Those murders, of course.'

'A gang job?' Pel asked.

'There was some problems over identification but they've discovered they were part of Tagliatti's mob.'

Pel frowned. He'd bumped into Maurice Tagliatti once before in the Miollis murder.* Not very seriously, though, and the death hadn't worried him much. When gangsters got themselves bumped off he didn't lose much sleep. It saved him a lot of trouble.

De Troq' had fished out one of the newspapers he'd brought with him. 'They've got their names now, though,' he said. 'Paul Richet, known as The Chinese, aged 42. Jean Epaulard, aged 23. Gérard Grimeaud, also 23. Jean Bernard, aged 19, known as La Petite Fleur. He was the runner for the gang. Marcel Bayon, 25. And Michel Cerbet, 39, known as Mick the Brick. It seems he used to be a bricklayer. Know them, Patron?'

'Not to my knowledge, thank God.'

'Covering all the usual interests. Pimping. Brothels. Protection rackets. It seems they were all at the bar when these three other types appeared in the doorway, one with the tommy gun, the other two with pistols. The landlord saw them coming in the doorway and dived behind the counter. Glasses, mirrors, bottles and chunks of bar went flying and when he lifted his head, four of them were dead. The other two were dead within an hour. No weapons have been found.'

Madame pulled a face and Pel had to apologise for their shop talk.

'What about the three gunmen? Any identities?'

'None at all. The police have their suspicions, of course.'

'Part of another gang?'

'Nobody knows yet and Tagliatti's not around for questioning. He's disappeared. His lawyer says he's in Switzerland doing a bit of tax dodging. On the other hand, it might be because the police want to interview him over that murder in Marseilles two years ago – type called De Fé, Boris de Fé. He was part of the upper crust, I believe.'

Pel sniffed and De Troq' continued enthusiastically. 'All the same, his business dealings were somewhat open to question, it seems, and he allowed his name to be used by a couple of dubious Paris types as collateral for a two-million franc loan to purchase a group of petrol stations.'

'Wasn't it accompanied by an insurance policy on De Fé's

* see PEL UNDER PRESSURE.

59

life?' Pel asked. 'So that when he was murdered the loan was paid off and a type called Hoff and his friends became sole owners of the group.'

'That's the case, Patron.'

'Was Tagliatti involved in that?'

'The Marseilles police think so. There's no proof, of course. There never is. And when the investigations got too close for comfort he went to ground. It won't stop him operating, of course. There are such things as telephones. Catching these three with the tommy gun's going to be tricky. Everybody has cast-iron alibis. Good ones, too. They can't be faulted.'

'Eye witnesses?'

'Not one.'

'What about the owner of the bar? And, from what I remember, there were other customers. And wasn't there a barmaid who had hysterics afterwards? And what about the old dear serving at the cigarette counter?'

'They swore they didn't see any faces.'

'Same old problem. Everybody scared to talk.'

'They said they were strangers.'

'From where?'

De Troq' looked up and smiled. 'Here, perhaps?' he suggested.

Pel was silent for a while and he noticed that Madame was watching with bright eyes. He could have sworn she was enjoying herself.

'Caceolari,' he said quietly. 'I'm going to set up a head-quarters in Beauregard's office. We'll do all our business there. But – ' he paused ' – we'll not put anything on paper and we'll not discuss anything there that we feel should be kept quiet. I don't trust the people on this island. Among them Beauregard. I also don't trust the telephone. It's still a hand-operated exchange and the operator listens in and could well be in somebody's pay.'

De Troq' nodded his approval.

'We shall make the Duponts' house the real headquarters,' Pel went on. 'You'll come for tea or coffee or a meal and we'll discuss the real business then.'

Madame beamed. 'Perhaps I can help. I learned shorthand when I was a girl. It'll give me something to do.'

60

'Very well,' Pel agreed. 'You can run the murder room.'

'What's a murder room?'

'Normally it has typewriters, files, telephones, card index systems, dozens of clerks and policemen, and Inspector Goriot to see it runs properly. Here, there'll be no files or card index systems. It'll consist chiefly of the kitchen table and your pen.'

Since the crime had occurred on the back doorstep of the Villa des Roses, its owner needed to be investigated in case he'd been running a criminal empire from one of the bedrooms, but he turned out to be an inoffensive English writer who'd bought the land five years before, built the villa for a holiday home, and hadn't been near the island for ages.

'He got diddled,' Beauregard said.

'I'll say he got diddled,' Pel said. 'Who was the builder?'

'Guy from the mainland. In prison at the moment for fiddling. The English type's still trying to get some of his money back.'

'I imagine,' Pel said dryly, 'that it will take some time.'

Since the owner could be written off at once, inevitably the Duponts were next on the list and it gave Pel enormous pleasure to have them in front of him in Beauregard's office.

'Why have we been brought here?' The wide encouraging smiles with which they had greeted Pel and his wife on their first evening on the island were conspicuous by their absence.

When Pel explained, Dupont exploded into tones of high dudgeon, as if he'd just been ejected by the police from a dubious night club. 'It's nothing to do with me!' he said. 'I've never been in trouble before! I've always been straightforward!'

'Always?' Pel asked silkily. 'Would it surprise you to know I'm considering sueing you for false pretences over a little matter of the Villa des Roses?'

Dupont simmered down abruptly but it was pretty obvious that, apart from letting badly aired, crumbling houses to chief inspectors of the Police Judiciaire and their new wives, he was not in the habit of indulging in criminal activities.

'Anybody else been in the house recently?' Pel asked coldly.

'Nobody.' Dupont glanced at his wife. 'We tried all last

61

season to let it,' he said sourly. 'But the word seems to get around. There were no takers.'

'Which will doubtless account for the dampness of the beds,' Pel said, 'and the fact that nothing worked.'

'It's the salt air,' Madame Dupont said. 'Having the sea on both sides. You could always air the beds by heating big pebbles from the beach in the oven, of course, and putting them between the sheets.'

Pel waved them away. They each had their own car – when they weren't being used by visiting chief inspectors and their wives, of course – had never called on Caceolari for transport, were obviously unconnected with the case and didn't seem to know anyone who might have been. 'I think you can go,' he said.

They still hadn't heard of the result of the autopsy on Caceolari and when they tried to find Doctor Nicolas, he was not at his home near Mortcerf, where they were greeted by the solitary occupant, a tatty-looking ginger cat, nor in the untidy surgery he ran in the Vieux Port. In the end they found him seated in one of the dozens of chairs set in rows outside the tourist bars near the harbour, with an empty glass in front of him.

He seemed to suffer like everybody else on the island except the Vicomte and his retinue from being unable to stand close enough to his razor, and a grey stubble darkened his cheeks. His moustache was stained yellow by the nicotine from the cigarette that hung permanently under his nose, and because it had the hollow sound of a grave about it, his cough was a warning to Pel that he ought to make another serious attempt to give up smoking. He didn't think he'd ever manage it, of course, because he'd already tried everything but acupuncture.

What the old doctor considered to be an autopsy didn't fit Pel's idea of one. The most that appeared to have been done was the tracing of the path of the wounds with a probe.

'There were four,' Nicolas said. 'Three at the back and one at the front. All done by a long-bladed knife no more than two centimetres wide. What Italians and vendettists call a stiletto.'

Because the season had still not got going, the expanse of

red, yellow and blue plastic chairs was not much occupied and they seemed lost in their centre. A few obvious holidaymakers clutched their beach umbrellas and sunbathing mats, their bags full of sunburn lotion, knitting and books. There were also a few youngsters along the harbour wall, all already as bronzed as Indians and wearing clothes that were remarkable chiefly for their raggedness. They seemed to work among the hired yachts and dinghies, and from their accents they were students who would be spending the summer pretending to work for holiday companies while, in fact, having a thoroughly enjoyable time whooping it up together.

Pel stared about him. It was a strange place to receive an autopsy report, and Doctor Nicolas was somewhat different from Doctor Minet who performed the duty in the city where Pel normally operated, who was precise, tidy and exact in details.

'His hands were gashed.' Doctor Nicolas held up his own hands, casually, indifferently, as if he didn't care very much whether it pleased or helped Pel or not. 'He'd obviously tried to grab the knife. Some of the wounds were deep. Since there was also blood inside the car and on the steering wheel, it seemed to me that someone had attacked him and he'd fought them off and made a dash for his car to try to get to you for help. The wounds in the back were superficial – as if they'd jabbed at him as he ran, and missed. The wound in the chest, which was doubtless the last one, was delivered, I would say, as he turned desperately to fight off his attacker. That was the wound that killed him. It was an upward thrust and went in just below the ribs and reached the heart.' He looked up. 'Do you want it all down on paper?'

'Yes.'

'Bon Dieu de bon Dieu! That's work!'

Pel studied the doctor. He had the sort of face that looked like a car that had been reassembled after an accident. Nothing matched and he looked seedy, while his clothes hung from him like a sack, his trousers, when he stood up, in danger, it seemed, of falling round his ankles.

'You seem to know your business,' he observed. 'Have you done this sort of thing before?'

'Many times.'

'I thought you didn't get that many murders here.'

'We don't. And if we did they'd be simple bludgeoning. A wife hitting a husband with a bottle when he came home drunk. A husband hitting his wife with a shovel when she nagged. Men trying to brain each other with jack handles. Fights. That sort of thing. Nothing so neat as this.'

'Then where did you do it?'

'Marseilles. I often worked for the police there.'

'Why did you come here?'

Nicolas indicated the brandy and soda he was drinking. 'That,' he said.

Pel eyed him for a moment. 'But is a knife as odd as you suggest? This place isn't far from Italy. Italians have a fondness for knives.'

'So do southern Frenchmen.' Nicolas gave a little cackle of laughter. 'They also use sisal spikes. Knives are forbidden but there's nothing to stop a man in a fight using one of those. They're as deadly as a dagger.'

'But on the whole they *don't* use them?'

Nicolas shrugged. 'The Vicomte keeps too sharp an eye on what goes on. If people cause trouble, they find their business fading. Nobody would come to their garage or their shop or their small holding.'

'He runs it like that, does he?'

The doctor gave Pel a glance under the brim of the battered straw hat. It was sly and boozy. 'It's as good a way of keeping order as I know,' he said.

Pel stared about him. The Place du Port, where they were sitting, was a concrete area as big as a football field. Around it were one or two boutique-type shops and the bars had a brash modernistic look that didn't fit the island or its architecture. They had plastic signs over the doors and plastic palms on the terrasses, and the rows of red, blue and yellow plastic-seated chairs, each bar's seating a different colour, were separated by alleyways to indicate territorial boundaries in a way that indicated a sort of organisation that was never, Pel felt sure, indigenous to the island. The seaward end of the square finished with a neat concrete wall with smart plastic benches, a flagpole, the harbourmaster's office, and a number of excellent jetties sticking out into the bay. Alongside the jetties were several smart yachts.

'The developers seem to have been hard at work here,' Pel

observed. 'This is a pretty modern set-up for a backward island of no known fame.'

Nicolas chuckled. 'It is a bit,' he agreed. 'But it'll be popular before long.'

'Somebody trying to push the place?'

'I suppose so.'

'Who paid for it?'

'I don't know. But when the smart yachts are moving up and down the Mediterranean in the summer and need to put in somewhere for the evening, they want somewhere where they can drink.'

'They can't eat,' Pel said, thinking of Riccio's.

Nicolas gave his low cackling laugh. It sounded like water going down a drain. 'Oh, they can in the summer. The hotel here in the Vieux Port puts on a splendid show. They also run a discotheque where everybody can have a jig together.' Nicolas smiled. 'You'd be surprised the sights we see here when the jet set arrive. You'd think they were dressed to go to the palace at Monaco or somewhere like that. And why not? This place's a bit like Monte Carlo. During the day, they wear scruffy jeans and striped shirts – expensive scruffy jeans and expensive striped shirts, mind you – but at night in their glad rags they set out to show us what they can do when they try.'

Pel gestured at the harbour. 'It's still a big affair.'

Nicolas shrugged. 'It's good for the island's trade.'

'Which, I suppose, is also the Vicomte's trade?'

'Put it that way if you like.'

'I'm surprised the government allowed it. It might be excellent for the jet set but it hardly fits in with the natural surroundings. Where did they get permission?'

'Usual place. The Ministry of Beaux Arts, I suppose. There's always plenty of this, isn't there?' Doctor Nicolas held out his hand and rubbed his thumb and forefinger together.

'Bribes?'

'It's been known.'

'Is the Vicomte involved in that sort of thing?'

Nicolas smiled. 'Shouldn't think so. He's no need to be. There are plenty of people here who'd be glad to sort out a little matter of that kind and present him with a fait accompli.'

'Would he accept it?'

'Wouldn't you?'

'Who're we thinking of in particular?'

'You won't find them in the Vieux Port. The Vieux Port's just islanders. People who've lived here for generations. You've got to look further afield than that.'

'How much further afield?'

'To the new developments. There *are* a few. There's one behind Biz and one behind Le Havre du Sud and one on the other coast at Muriel. That's a good one. A big one. They bought the land – '

'Who from?'

Nicolas shrugged. 'It must have been the Vicomte. It's his island. They laid down roads and dropped their plans in the offices of house agents on the mainland. Almost every plot was bought up at once.'

'Did the Vicomte object?'

'He sold the land. How could he?'

'And who was behind this project?'

'Type called Rambert. Raymond Rambert. He lives there. He fancies himself a bit, I think. House as big as the Elysée Palace. Tough. Always a woman there. Does his business on the telephone like the film people. Never face to face. Never anything on paper.'

'Would *he* know Caceolari?'

'I expect so.'

'Did you?'

Dr Nicolas was toying with his empty glass now, dropping clear hints that he needed another. Pel gestured at the waiter and neither of them spoke until the fresh brandy had arrived. Nicolas swallowed half of it at a gulp.

'What sort of man was he?'

'Lazy.' Nicolas gestured. 'Half the time his taxi didn't work.'

'It didn't when it picked us up from the boat.'

'Exactly. There's only one bus on the island. It runs from the Vieux Port here to Biz three times a week, and to Le Havre du Sud the other three days. On Sunday it doesn't run at all. Caceolari's was the only taxi and you'd therefore assume he'd do well. But he didn't. There are no petrol pumps on the island and all cars have to be filled by hand

66

from cans at the garage here.' A limp hand waved. 'At the other end of the town over there. I've seen holidaymakers with villas at Biz who've missed the bus after shopping here in the Vieux Port wait hours for Caceolari's taxi to turn up. And when it has turned up, it's had to coast down the hill because he's run out of petrol. They've then waited another half hour while he fetched a can of petrol from the garage and then, having filled it, they've had to push-start it because the battery was flat.'

'You'd say he was inefficient?'

Nicolas lit a cigarette. 'Everybody's inefficient here. The fishing fleet's inefficient, and out of date. Caceolari's taxi was out of date. Apart from the new one here in the Vieux Port the hotels are out date. The police are out of date. The fire brigade's out of date. I'm out of date. The only thing that isn't out of date's the Vicomte's estate. That runs like clockwork.'

'To the detriment of the rest of the place?'

Nicolas finished his brandy, and Pel gestured again at the waiter. For the first time Nicolas was talking freely.

'No,' he admitted. 'If if weren't for the Vicomte the whole damn place would die under our feet. People in the south are always lazy. It's the sun. It's possible to live without money.' He gestured at the youngsters arguing noisily on the sea wall. 'That's why *they* come here. They don't get paid much but they can live like lords. They don't need clothes. Food's cheap. Drink's cheap. In the summer the place's full of them. All sleeping rough. On the beach. In boats. Sharing apartments. Twelve to a room. But they go away in the winter. The Vicomte's freezers employ *islanders* and his export business employs a whole lot more. All year round. Frozen food, olives, cheese – island cheese. Olive oil, flowers. To the mainland for the Marseilles shops.'

'What about imports?'

'Food, of course. Pasta from Italy. The people here have Italian backgrounds and they like pasta. Italian wine. It's cheap. Fruit from southern Italy. Machinery of one sort or another.'

'What's "one sort or another"?'

Nicolas gave his low chuckle. 'Juke boxes. Pin tables. All the bars have them and youngsters don't seem able to live without them. Coffee machines.'

'Small ones?'

'Rapido Minis. Rapidos are the same as Espressos or Gaggias really. Minis are smaller editions. The Vicomte brings them in. He buys them half-completed, adds the motors and the wiring in workshops he's made in the stables at the back of the château and sells them complete on the mainland. Half the bars along the south coast have them. And half the houses have the miniature. I've got one myself in my surgery. You simply switch on and it starts working. He must be making a fortune from the fact that people have grown too lazy even to make a cup of coffee.'

'How many do they need on an island this size?'

'Not many.' As Nicolas pushed his glass forward, the waiter filled it automatically, and Pel began to suspect the old doctor passed out every afternoon in the heat of the sun. 'But Roche-mare's clever. He imports them via Corsica, which is close by. That way, he dodges a lot of the duties on them. We make our own laws here, you know. Like Monaco, San Marino and Andorra. And we're not too hard on smugglers because there used to be a lot here. There still are, I suppose. Watches from Switzerland, whisky from Scotland. There used to be pirates, too. Perhaps there still are.'

'Pirates?'

'Pirates were people who took over islands where they lived out of reach of the law, spending their ill-gotten loot. We have a few here like that. They made their money on the mainland then came here to spend it.'

Pel was silent for a while then he brought the subject back to Caceolari. 'If Caceolari thought he was in grave danger, as he must have been when he was attacked, why did he try to get to the Villa des Roses? Why did he climb the hill out of the town and rattle through all those olive groves, knowing that every minute he delayed increased the risk of dying? He must have known that when he arrived he'd still have to get out of his car and scramble down that scree slope. Why didn't he just go to the police station? It's over there.'

As Pel gestured at the drab flat-fronted building at the opposite side of the square, Nicolas' boozy smile came again.

'Perhaps there was a whole line of people barring his way,' he suggested.

Or else, Pel thought to himself, he didn't expect to get much help from Beauregard.

8

It was Babin, the postman, who informed them cheerfully that a house near Biz had been burned to the ground during the night. He was off-duty and riding a blue two-stroke motor cycle. Stopping outside the Duponts' house where Pel and his wife were sitting on the verandah drinking their coffee, he tossed a bundle of catalogues into the garage. Since the pile never grew larger, they assumed the Duponts sneaked in when they were out and removed them.

'Thought I'd drop them in,' he said. 'We don't work union rules on the island. Heard about the burning?'

He explained what had happened. 'Up on the cliffs,' he said. 'Overlooking the sea. One of those new conversions they did two years ago. I went out with the mail and there it was. Gone. Owners in Paris, of course. They'll probably not find out for days. I noticed one or two round there looking for what they could get.'

'One or two who?'

'Neighbours. Islanders. Looting, you'd call it, I expect. I bet the garden tools have vanished. They probably vanished before they even set fire to the place.'

'Is that what happens?'

The postman shrugged. 'I expect the owners have plenty of money.'

'Perhaps they haven't,' Pel said. 'Perhaps they'd saved up all their lives to build a holiday home here.'

The postman grinned. 'Not they. I know them. They come here for August and let the place in May, June, July and September to a British holiday firm. They've made what it cost them to buy and modernise it ten times over already.'

'Are you an islander?'

'Born and bred.'

'I thought you might be.'

70

Babin waved, revved his engine and let in the clutch. The motor bike lifted on to its rear wheel as he shot off towards the harbour.

'Very modern, this island,' Pel commented dryly.

They'd left it to Beauregard to see Madame Caceolari, the dead man's widow, in the belief that, since she knew him, it might be easier. Interviewing the spouses of murder victims was never a job any policeman sought and, since Beauregard had so far done remarkably little, they'd decided it was a chore he might well undertake. Instead he informed them he'd been too busy.

'Doing what?' Pel snapped.

Beauregard gestured. 'You'd be surprised at the paperwork.'

Every policeman knew it took longer to fill in the papers afterwards than to arrest a criminal, but so far nobody had been arrested and the island seemed a remarkably easy-going place, so there couldn't have been a lot for Beauregard to do. But he was full of excuses, his attitude that of the only righteous man in a perfidious and dissolute world, so that Pel began to wonder if he'd been carrying on an affair with Madame Caceolari or something, and they decided to go themselves. Enough time had surely elapsed for her to collect herself and, with De Troq' driving the Duponts' car, they left Madame chattering happily in the kitchen to Nelly Biazz and headed towards the old town.

Caceolari's wife was a plump pale woman who looked as though she avoided the sun as much as possible. Like so many of the islanders, she looked more Italian than French and had obviously once been pretty. But too much pasta had put on flesh, and she had become heavy-footed, hollow-eyed and slow.

She showed Pel and De Troq' into a dark kitchen where she sat them at a table covered with American cloth in a hideous red and green squared pattern. It was old, frayed at the edges and marked with knife cuts which had gone black with age. The sink was piled with dirty crockery and the Butane gas cooker was thick with grease. As they sat down, she placed in front of them glasses that were thick and opaque enough to have been in the family for generations and become worn with use. Sloshing wine into them, she sat opposite and waited with her hands on the table for them to speak. Despite what Beauregard had said, she looked remarkably composed.

After the formalities of sympathy and condolences, they got down to the questions.

'My Paolo was a good man,' she said. 'But he was weak. He was lazy.'

'Did he ever quarrel with anybody?'

'He never quarrelled. Not even with me. It was frustrating. When I wanted to quarrel with him – and that was often because he made me angry – he simply refused.'

'Then who'd want to kill him?'

She shrugged.

'Had he any enemies you know of?'

She shrugged again. 'He was too lazy to make enemies. He needed strength. *Strength*.' she clasped one of her hands into a fist and held it up. 'Strength,' she said again.

'Can you explain, Madame?'

'He didn't like work. He wouldn't repair his taxi. He preferred to sit in the sunshine and talk. Drink, too. Then, when someone wanted his taxi, it wouldn't go and he lost the fare. Always I had to tell him to work on it. Always I had to remind him there was work to do, people to be fetched and carried, repairs to be made.' She gestured at the kitchen. 'Look at this. It needs painting. I need a new cooker. I need curtains. I need a new covering for the table. Did I get them? No. And I never will now. It's a good job there are no children. I think he was too lazy even for that.'

'He was out the night he was killed,' Pel said. 'Did you know he was out?'

'He was never in. If he wasn't drinking by the harbour, he was drinking at Biz. If he wasn't at Biz, he was at Le Havre du Sud. Or with Magimel, who has a farm in the hills at Crêvecoeur. Or Lesage who runs the garage, or Rolland who has the forge, or Desplanques.'

'And Desplanques?'

'He runs the olive oil factory for the Vicomte.'

'On the night he was killed he was at Mortcerf.'

'With that woman? I thought so. It's understandable.'

'Understandable? Why?'

'Because she's a woman. She has pretty clothes, such as I

72

don't have. She has a better figure. She's not worn out with work as I am. She has money. I haven't. She offered him drink. I never did. He was always there. Every week he went.'

'He was there the week before, too, I believe.'

'I expect he was. I didn't bother to ask him. I went my own way. I go over to his sister's for company. She's Madame Oudry, who lives in Biz. I go over a lot. Two or three times a week. We get on well. We always have, because her husband's another of the same sort. Shifty, lazy. Up to things.'

'What sort of things?'

'He gambles. There's somewhere they hold cockfights. He's the baker for Biz but he has a boat and prefers to go fishing. I think he fetches American cigarettes from Italy occasionally. On the quiet. There's never enough bread in Biz because he's always too busy doing other things.'

'How did you get to Biz? It's a fair distance. Did your husband drive you there?'

'Him? He was always too busy doing nothing. I've got a motor scooter. It's only small and I have to pedal up the hills a bit, but it takes me around. How else would I get there? You wouldn't catch me walking across the cliffs. There are adders. I only go when Oudry's working or away, anyway. I don't like him. He drinks too much.'

'Did he drink with your husband?'

'No. He drinks with Maquin, the cooper at the olive oil plant, or with Turidu Riccio, the fisherman who keeps the restaurant on the harbour. They're as thick as thieves.'

'What about the night your husband was killed? Had you been to Biz that night?'

'No. I stayed home. He was watching the television. He told me he'd met a detective. You, I suppose. Then he said he had to go out. I knew he was going out for a drink.' She paused. 'I was out the previous week,' she volunteered. 'The previous time when he went to Mortcerf. I wanted to know where he'd been and he told me. He was so late. It was late when *I* came back and I thought he'd be in bed. But his car was out and I thought, "There's a moon." The moon always affects him. He becomes romantic and goes to see that woman at Mortcerf. He arrived home the next morning when it was already becoming daylight. He must have stayed with her. She's that sort, they say.'

Pel frowned. 'He wasn't at Mortcerf all that time,' he said. 'He left at midnight. Are you sure of the time he came back?'

'I heard his taxi. I can recognise it. Everybody in the island knows it because of the noise it made. The exhaust needed repairing and it sounded like a tank arriving. It would be about four o'clock.'

'So, if he left Mortcerf at midnight, where was he until four o'clock?'

'Drinking somewhere, I expect. He usually was.'

Outside again, sitting in the car, Pel looked at De Troq'.

'There are four hours missing somewhere that night,' he said.

'Where was he during that time? Let's go and check on his movements with these drinking friends of his.'

They tried the garage first. Lesage, the proprietor, was a small man with a face like a ferret, who wore overalls so ingrained with grease they looked as if they'd stand up by themselves. By means of a rusty-looking funnel he was filling an ancient van driven by a man who was obviously a farmer, using cans as Luigi André had said, which he had to fill from a drum by means of a pump. He stopped long enough to tell them he saw Caceolari most weeks, either to fill his taxi or to have a drink with him.

As the farmer drove off, he put down the can he was using, tapped the drum to make sure it was empty and began to roll another in its place.

'I'm thinking of installing an electric pump,' he announced proudly. 'Save all this work. I run the fire brigade here and there are always things to see to, so I don't have much time.'

'Caceolari,' Pel said. 'Did he have any enemies?'

'None that I knew of.'

'Nobody who'd want to get rid of him?'

Lesage shrugged. 'Only his wife.'

'When did you last see him?'

'About two days before he was killed, I think. He came for petrol. We had a drink in the bar there.' Lesage gestured towards the alley behind the garage where they could see a red, white and blue striped blind.

'How did he seem?'

'Bit worried, I thought.'

74

'What about?'

'He didn't say, but it must have been important because he talked of going to see someone.'

'Who? A lawyer?'

'We haven't got any here. But I think he did see someone, I saw him later and he said he'd got nowhere.'

'Who would he see? Beauregard?'

Lesage gave a grin. 'Him? I wouldn't tell *him* anything.' He held out his hand and rubbed his finger and thumb together. 'He'd want some of this before he did anything.'

'Well, who then?'

'Somebody at the château, perhaps. They know more about what goes on than most people. Perhaps that was it. They're usually helpful if people get into trouble. I'll say that.'

'This worry of his – '

Lesage shrugged. 'I don't know. Perhaps he was short of money. He sometimes was. Especially just before the season started – this sort of time – and he had nothing after the winter. It was always better when the holidaymakers came because they were always losing themselves and getting farmers to telephone for him to come and fetch them. Or else the motor bikes they hired broke down. I think Caceolari had an arrangement with young Rabillard, who hires them out. At least they always seemed to have his telephone number. Perhaps Rabillard gave it to them with the bikes and Caceolari gave him a cut on the fare he collected for taking them home.'

They told him they were looking for a farmer called Magimel and would he know where his farm was?

Lesage scratched his head. 'Why didn't you talk to him when he was here?'

'Who?'

'Magimel. That was him who just drove off in the van.'

Pel looked at De Troq' and sighed. 'Never mind. We'll find him later.'

They found Rolland sweating over his forge. He was a big man in the manner of Riccio, the fisherman who ran the restaurant, wearing a leather apron and beating at a red-hot horseshoe.

'There are still a few horses in the hills,' he said. 'And a few mules too. They keep me going.' He gestured at the walls.

'I also repair ploughs, rakes and harrows, and bits of tractor. When I've got time I make wrought-iron things. Gates. Plantpot holders for hanging on the walls.' He grinned. 'You'd be surprised how many I sell to the people who have holiday homes here. People from the north all seem to think that in the Mediterranean you have to have the outside of the house dripping with geraniums.'

'Caceolari,' Pel prompted.

Rolland whacked the horseshoe a couple of times and straightened up. 'They say he was stabbed,' he said.

'He was. Several times. Do you know anybody who'd have reason to do that?'

'Caceolari? Everybody liked Caceolari.' Rolland grinned. 'Except when they ordered his taxi and it wouldn't start.'

He hadn't recently been drinking with Caceolari at all because his wife had been unwell for some time and, in any case, he didn't believe in staying up late. It must have been Desplanques he was with, he said. *He* liked to stay up late.

But it wasn't Desplanques either. They had to get Tissandi's permission to see him but the estate manager gave them carte blanche to enter the factory and, standing in front of the black corrugated iron sheds where the island's olives were crushed and the oil purified, Desplanques explained that he hadn't seen Caceolari for around a fortnight.

'What about the night of the 13th? To be exact, the early hours of the 14th?'

Desplanques shook his head. He'd been attending a christening that day in Le Havre du Sud.

'My grandson,' he said. 'We stayed there all night because we drank quite a bit. My son runs the Solmar Hotel there. Good job. Good wages. It's a good hotel. Not as good as the hotel in the Vieux Port here, but good. He can afford a good do. He married Fleurie's daughter. Of course Fleurie wasn't there. He ran off with Pinchon's wife. But Madame Fleurie was there. You'll have met her? The Black Widow.'

'While you were in Le Havre du Sud,' Pel asked, 'did you see Caceolari? Would he perhaps have taken any of the guests there in his taxi?'

No, Desplanques hadn't seen Caceolari in Le Havre du Sud. The Solemar Hotel was actually just outside, near the only beach in that part of the island, and, in any case, every-body came in their own car.

'My son's friends are important people,' Desplanques said proudly. 'They *all* have their own cars. Well – ' he shrugged ' – some of them use the vans or pick-ups they use for their work, and Quérard actually came in a lorry. But then he would, wouldn't he? He has no sense of occasion.'

'And in any case,' he ended, 'for the time you're talking of, after midnight into the early hours, they'd all be asleep. I was, anyway. My son put me to bed. It was a good christening.'

Le Havre du Sud turned out to be no more than a tiny village round a minute harbour where more bronzed students were busy painting rowing boats and pedalos ready for the season. The houses were white and there seemed to be only one grocery store, known, despite the fact that it was no bigger than a garage, as the Supermarket du Sud. There were the usual holiday apartments and houses, most of them still empty, several gift shops, still not open, and three bars, all far from busy. The bars were the obvious place to ask but nobody had seen Caceolari during the evening of young Desplanques' christening, of which they'd all been well aware because of the noise it engendered, and because it was out of season, and most of them had been invited and had closed early.

They got exactly the same sort of answers in Biz.

It took them what seemed hours to find Magimel. People were willing enough to direct them to his farm at Crêvecoeur but, since none of the roads had signs on them to Crêvecoeur, it was difficult to follow their directions. Studying the few they came across, it occurred to Pel that there seemed to be an obsession with unhappiness on the island. L'Aride. Mortcerf. Crêvecoeur. Amorperdu. Désolair. The Barren Land. Dead deer. Broken heart. Lost love. Woebegone. Perhaps it had some connection with the fact that it was impossible to identify the roads; judging by their own difficul-ties, there must have been quite a few woebegone lost lovers with broken hearts trying to find their way around. Perhaps they killed the deer to avoid starving.

Eventually they found a stone-built place on the slope of a hill. It's name, Pel was not surprised to notice, was Aventure

Désespérée – Forlorn Hope. The islanders really did have a thing about gloom.

There were a few crops, a few olives, a broken harrow, a few chickens, a vine over the back porch showing its first grapes, and a dog that barked at them as if it had gone off its head. As De Troq' swung his foot threateningly at it, it bolted, yelling blue murder.

'Mustn't threaten dogs,' Pel rebuked mildly, affected by the warmth of the day. 'If a blind man's wooden leg explodes nobody gives a damn, but kick a dog and you're ostracised for life.'

Magimel had appeared at the noise. 'I saw you down in the Vieux Port,' he said as they explained their errand. 'Why didn't you ask me when you saw me at the garage.'

'Because I didn't know then that you were Magimel.'

'Oh!' Magimel nodded as if he saw the wisdom of that. 'Yes,' he went on. 'Caceolari came here.'

They had finally drawn blood but there didn't appear to be much of it.

'He stayed late,' Magimel said. 'He didn't leave until the early hours of the morning.'

'The early hours?' Pel stared. 'He couldn't have. He was killed – on my doorstep – long before then.'

'Not *that* night!' Magimel looked at Pel as if he weren't quite right in the head. 'Not the night he was killed. The other night.'

'Which other night?'

'The other night he came.'

Pel glared. 'Which night was that.'

'The night of those shootings in Nice. We sat in the kitchen and split a bottle of wine. Well, perhaps it was two. We sometimes did – and he stayed later than usual. We got talking about the shootings. Six of them. Smeared across the bar counter. A tommy gun, they said. It was on the radio. They were making a lot of it. We talked about it.'

'Why? Did you think there might be some connection between the island and the shooting?'

Magimel looked indignant. 'We don't go in for that sort of thing here,' he said. 'An occasional fist fight perhaps. That's all. We don't use weapons here.'

'Only knives,' Pel reminded him. 'Such as killed Caceolari.'

'Yes – well – but that's just the Italian lot.'

'Who're the Italian lot?'

'The people who've got Italian blood in them. From the days when this place belonged to Italy.'

'And who're they?'

Magimel thought about it for some time. 'Well, most of us,' he admitted.

'What time did Caceolari leave this night you're talking about?'

'About two in the morning. My wife made it very clear it was time he pushed off. She kept banging on the floor of the bedroom. It's over the kitchen and she's got a bad leg and uses a stick, so she can make a hell of a racket. In the end he decided he'd better go. But one of his headlights had fallen off and the other wasn't working because the bulb had gone and he'd also run out of petrol. But he wasn't worried. It was all downhill to his house and he knew the roads round the island like the creases on the back of his hand. And in any case the moon was bright enough to read the paper. He left finally about 2.30.'

'How long would it take him to get home then?'

'Half an hour at the outside, going dead slow.'

'So where was he between 2.30.a.m. and when his wife heard him stop outside his house as it was growing daylight?' Pel asked. 'It's my guess that night will tell us as much about the night he was killed as when he was found on my doorstep. If he disappeared into thin air for an hour or more, there must have been a good reason.' He looked at a list of times he'd written on the back of an envelope. 'He was with the Robles woman at Mortcerf until around midnight, then, because he fancied a few more drinks, he called on Magimel. That was normal enough but this time he stayed longer than usual because they started discussing that shooting in Marseilles. He left about 2.30 and should have arrived home at 3.a.m. So where did he go after that?'

Sitting at the kitchen table in the Duponts' house, with Madame Pel watching bright-eyed from the other side, they studied the map of the island. Beauregard had been unable to provide one – 'We've never needed one,' he said. 'Everybody's lived here all their lives' – so they'd had to buy one at the newspaper shop in the Vieux Port which sold magazines – usually out of date; books – usually dog-eared from being handled and rejected; foreign paperbacks, most of them from an era long past; cheap plastic toys for children, cottons, wool, writing paper, pencils, and ball-point refills. The map was as dog-eared as the books and was one of a number the proprietor had bought for the tourists who were in the habit of getting as lost on their hired bicycles and lightweight motor-cycles as Pel and De Troq' had in their search for Magimel.

It was printed in gaudy colours and showed no contours, but the high points and the views worth seeing, of which there seemed to be remarkably few, were marked with a star. They managed to pinpoint Magimel's farm, not without difficulty because the map showed only the main roads and none of the by-roads, and they began to trace Caceolari's route from the Vieux Port to Mortcerf, then to Magimel's farm and back to his home. The road ended above the harbour.

'I was up there this morning,' Madame Pel said. 'It's only a few minutes walk. I sat under the trees. It's shady and there's a beautiful view. You can see right down to the sea. Someone waved to me and I waved back.' She looked at Pel. 'Perhaps he stopped there before he went home. Perhaps the moon encouraged him. It would be as bright as day because full moon was that week.'

'He was only a quarter of a mile from his home,' Pel pointed out. 'Surely he wouldn't stop at three in the morning within such a short distance of his bed to look at a view he'd seen hundreds of times before.'

'Perhaps he – well, he'd had a lot to drink – perhaps he had to stop. Men do, you know. I've seen them. Standing under the trees with their backs to the road.'

Pel looked quickly at his wife. 'Within two minutes of home?' he asked.

'Or – ' De Troq's head jerked up suddenly ' – or else, in that moon we're talking about, he saw something down there by the harbour that caught his interest and he stopped to watch. Something illegal, perhaps.'

'Wouldn't they see *him*? Or hear his car?'

'Why should they, Patron? They wouldn't hear him

because the engine wasn't running. He had no petrol and he coasted down the hill from Magimel's place. And they wouldn't see him because he only had one light and the bulb in that was gone. They'd never suspect there was a car up there with a man in it watching them.'

It suddenly began to seem a possibility. Pel patted his wife's hand.

'You'll make a detective yet,' he said and she seemed delighted with the compliment.

9

Pel and De Troq' were watching from the bar with Beauregard as Caceolari's body was carried along the harbour. The funeral was a quiet affair and there was no hearse because there wasn't a hearse on the island. Coffins were always carried on the shoulders of relatives and when someone living in the hills died, they were brought to the Vieux Port in the backs of pickup trucks, specially scrubbed and decorated with black crêpe for the occasion.

Behind the coffin was Madame Caceolari in a heavy veil, helped along by a youth and another woman in a black shawl, and followed by a tall pasty-faced man. There was only a sprinkling of mourners, among them, Pel noticed, the tall burly Tissandi, the Vicomte's manager, and Ignazi, the limp youth who acted as his secretary, who, he supposed, were there to represent the Vicomte.

Because of the steeply rising ground behind the harbour, the church was set high above the sea wall and the priest was standing at the top of the steps dressed in a cream cope and a green and gold stole. They looked important and even new and, in that little community, splendid.

'The Vicomte helps keep the church nice.' Beauregard gave the explanation. 'He gives a lot towards its upkeep.'

The bearers, they noticed, included Lesage, Magimel, Rolland and Desplanques.

'His pals from the Vieux Port,' Beauregard said.

They watched the little procession climb the steps to the church, the boots of the bearers fumbling carefully for a firm foothold. The door had been hung with black drapes decorated with silver braid and the priest raised his hand in blessing before turning to lead the cortège inside.

'The rest all relatives?' Pel asked.

Beauregard shook his head. 'He didn't have that many.

The graveyard's just behind. There's a family tomb. Mother and father there. The coffin doesn't come back down here. Too tricky. About twenty years ago, one of the bearers stumbled and the whole lot crashed to the bottom.' Beauregard seemed to find it amusing. 'The coffin burst open and one of the bearers broke a leg. He sued. So did the dead man's family. It would have bankrupted the Holy Father in Rome, the sums they asked. They said the steps were crooked and too steep and had winter lichen on them. As usual the Vicomte sorted it out and he had a door put in the church off the south side of the nave. You can go through there now straight to the churchyard. It makes it a lot easier.'

'I can see it would.' Pel agreed. 'Is there another way into the churchyard apart from through the church?'

Beauregard pointed to a winding set of stone steps. 'Up there,' he said. 'Originally they used to have to come back down the church steps and then up there to get to the churchyard. I was told it led to all sorts of capers because sometimes the bearers had had a few drinks.'

They found their way into the churchyard, a shabby little patch as run down as the rest of the old part of the town, and waited under the tall cypresses for the procession to emerge. A gravedigger eyed them curiously as he leaned against one of the square family mausoleums.

As the coffin reappeared, it was led by the priest, who, Pel noticed, was wearing rubber goloshes over his boots, and was followed by Madame Caceolari still supported by the woman and the youth.

'Who're those two?' he asked.

'That's his sister Denise,' Beauregard said. 'And her son, his nephew. He's a chef at the hotel in the Vieux Port.'

'What about the pasty-faced type behind?'

'That's his brother-in-law, Albert Oudry, the baker. He married Caceolari's sister.'

Because it was handy and it was growing late, they telephoned Madame Pel and went to Riccio's for lunch. Riccio met them as usual, his big hands black from the charcoal he'd been placing on the grill. Wiping his fingers carefully on his white apron, he shook hands and showed them to a scrubbed wooden table. Placing a wine glass containing one wilting flower in the centre, he followed it with three more empty ones and a carafe of white wine. 'Drink, Monsieur?'

'How do you know,' Pel asked tartly, 'that we shan't be drinking red?'

'Because Monsieur will be eating fish.'

'Will we? Why?'

'Because there's only fish on the menu, Monsieur. Swordfish. Frozen. It's very good, though.'

Madame looked as though she would have preferred to get up and leave.

As Riccio stoked up his stove and produced a salad containing nuts, onions and celery, they got on to the question of the fish.

'There seems to be an extraordinary number of swordfish round here,' Madame observed stiffly.

'Well, not really,' Riccio said apologetically from the stove. 'Plenty of the other kind, though.'

'Which, unfortunately, you don't have.'

'Well, actually, the fishing's not been good this spring. Normally, it's very good.'

Madame seemed to be growing a little annoyed and Pel tried to bring the tension down from boiling point. 'How often do you go?'

Riccio shrugged. 'When the tourists start coming, I have to look after the restaurant. The last time was a fortnight ago. I went out in the afternoon and came back early the next morning.'

'Catch much?'

Riccio smiled over his shoulder. '*That* was a good trip. We had a good catch.'

'Then why is there none for us?' Madame Pel demanded sharply.

Riccio smiled. 'Everybody likes fish, Madame.'

'Don't you freeze any of it?' Pel asked.

'It gets eaten too quickly. There's never any left.'

After the fiasco over the fish, Madame decided to treat De Troq' that evening to a meal of her own cooking – complete with all the trimmings.

Unfortunately, when they headed for the shops in the early

evening they found them locked, bolted and barred. An old man sitting on the sea wall in the sunshine explained.

'Gone shooting, I expect,' he said.

Pel stared round them. Every shop in the town seemed to have closed. 'All of them?'

'Everybody round here goes at this time of the year. I would, too, if I were younger.'

Sure enough they could hear occasional fusillades from among the trees on the hills behind the town.

'What do they shoot?'

'Pigeons, Monsieur. They come over in thousands from North Africa about this time of the year so everybody shoots them. To protect the crops. They're a menace and everybody goes. Even the Vicomte. He lets Maquin, his cooper, have the day off because he's such a good shot.'

'So when will the shops open?'

'They won't. Everybody did their shopping at lunchtime.'

'Why?'

'Because they knew everybody would be going shooting.'

'How did they know that?'

'Well, they'll have gone shooting, too.'

In a strange sort of way it made sense.

The old man prayed passionately as Pel dropped a coin in his hand that the saints might give him success, and they decided they'd eat instead at the hotel in the Vieux Port which, since it could be called on at any time to cater for a boatload of yachtsmen – even perhaps a whole *flotilla* of them from one of the sailing holiday organisations that infested the Mediterranean these days – would be unlikely to have its staff out shooting pigeons. They also decided that Nelly should join them and Nelly, her eyes on De Troq', was more than delighted.

The hotel was a lavish place and it was easy to see why it was popular with the people with money who came to the island in the summer with their boats. The bar counter was covered with cowhides, as were all the chairs and stools, and there were more cowhides hanging on the wall. A whole herd must have been slaughtered to decorate the place.

'From Spain,' the barman said proudly. 'They use them a lot there. It's easy to get to Majorca from here and we got the idea from a hotel there.'

85

'*Who* got the idea?' Pel asked.

'The boss, I suppose.'

'And who would that be?'

'Rambert, I suppose. He's one of them. They put the place up two years ago. To catch the yacht trade.'

They ate on the terrasse under an awning of vines. The meal was good and had class in an international manner, but Pel was thinking about other things. When his wife reproved him he started to life and gestured.

'I was looking round,' he admitted. 'This place doesn't fit in with the rest of the island very well, does it? It's modern. It's like the harbour – it sticks out like a sore thumb. I keep wondering how they got permission for it. The Ministry of Beaux Arts is very sticky about that sort of thing these days. France isn't like Spain and Italy where they stick these things up everywhere so fast they fall down the next year.'

'You think there might have been a little – ?' De Troq' worked his finger and thumb together.

'There seems to be a lot of it about,' Pel said. 'Perhaps it's catching.'

There was another burning in the night. They heard the fire brigade go past the house in the early hours and even saw the glow of the flames over the trees on the hill.

'Belonged to a fabric manufacturer from Lyons,' Babin, the postman, told them the next morning when he delivered his daily quota of pamphlets for the Duponts. 'Nice place. But he had a lot of money, so I suppose it would be, wouldn't it? He spent a small fortune on it. Overlooks the sea towards Corsica. Smashing views. There wasn't much left of it.'

'Did *you* see it burning?' Pel said.

'No. It started during the night. But I know the place. I deliver to Magimel who lives near there and he's always sending for catalogues and seeds and his wife's gone nuts on this mail-order business. Buys half of what she wants by mail.'

Beauregard seemed to be considering the arson with his usual unruffled calm. 'Nobody knew a thing,' he said.

'Do you have any suspects?'

'No.'

'Somebody ought to have.' Pel already had a suspicion but

it wasn't his affair and he knew his interference wouldn't be welcomed.

De Troq' found out who had financed the building of the harbour simply by buying drinks for the manager of the hotel in the Vieux Port.

'Rambert,' he said. 'This type we keep hearing about. It's a consortium but Rambert's the one who runs it. Comes from Marseilles and has a house at Muriel, that development area at the other side of the island. He comes in regularly with a yacht. He's a financier. One of those who don't seem to do any work except from their yachts. Worth a fortune.'

'And who bribed the officials in the Ministry of Beaux Arts?'

'That, Patron,' De Troq' admitted, 'I haven't found out yet. I suspect it'll take a little longer. Miracles do. And it *will* be a miracle if we find that one out. However, there is one interesting little point. I learned that our friend Rambert's related to – guess who? – our friend Hoff, who was involved in that little deal over the Paris petrol stations. You'll remember it was all investigated after that type, Boris de Fé, was murdered in Marseilles. They got nothing on Hoff but he turned out to be rather a dubious type.'

'Now that's interesting,' Pel agreed. 'Let's get on to Paris and have them dig around a bit and see if they can find out who Hoff's friends are. They might turn out to be interesting, too.'

Even if there had been corruption over the building of the harbour and the hotel – and it looked very much as though there might have been – somehow it didn't seem likely to be what had worried Caceolari. Nevertheless, it was becoming fairly obvious that he'd seen something he shouldn't have seen and it seemed important to have another talk with his wife, to find out if he'd ever let anything slip which might indicate more to them.

Madame Caceolari was surprised to see them back, but she went through the same rigmarole as before without turning a hair. Bang went the bottle to the table, bang-bang-bang went the glasses, then she sat down, her fingers entwined, and waited for them to speak.

'When your husband came back on the morning of the 14th.,' Pel said, ' did he say where he'd been? After he left Mortcerf.'

'He said he'd been with Magimel.'

'He left Magimel's at 2.30. Did he say whether he'd been anywhere else?'

'He said he'd had trouble with his car.'

'Well, he had no petrol. And no lights. He came down from Magimel's on the car's own momentum. Did he say he'd stopped anywhere?'

'No.'

'Did he say he'd seen anything?'

'Only Riccio's boat coming in. He'd been fishing.'

'Well, Riccio said he was out that night so it's likely. But how did he know it was Riccio?'

'It was moonlight and they've all got numbers. And Riccio has the only yellow boat in the harbour. All the others are blue or green or red. It's there for you to see. Anybody can see it. It hasn't been out of the harbour since. I suppose Riccio had been out with his pals.'

'Which pals? Did your husband say?'

'He said he saw Maquin, the cooper at the olive oil plant.'

'Did he see the catch?'

'He said he saw them carrying it ashore to the restaurant. It looked heavy. As if they'd had a good trip.'

'Did he say what sort of fish they were.'

'He couldn't see. He said they had it wrapped in canvas. He saw them put it inside Riccio's place. Then they locked up again and left. I expect they went somewhere to do some drinking to celebrate.'

'At *that* hour?'

'It's nothing for Riccio.'

'Have *you* eaten recently at Riccio's?'

'The islanders don't. He charges too much. Tourist prices. We notice it.'

Pel had noticed it, too.

'Besides,' Madame Caceolari went on, 'he's only just opened. Two or three days ago. Just after my husband was murdered. He's been painting. Getting ready for the season.'

'What about the following days? Did your husband behave normally?'

'Well, he seemed worried. But he always worried a bit when he was short of money. Or because his taxi wouldn't work. Or because he couldn't afford a new battery. Things like that.'

'Did he go on being worried?'

She considered for a moment. 'Come to think of it, he didn't have much to say.'

'Would you say he had something on his mind? He seemed a cheerful enough type, from what I hear.'

Yes, it seemed that Caceolari *had* seemed different. Quieter than usual. Once he'd mentioned Beauregard. 'He seemed to want to talk to him. But he kept putting it off. I wondered if he'd been mixed up in something.'

'What sort of something?'

'Well, there's only one sort of thing to get mixed up in here. Smuggling.'

'Had he ever been involved in anything like that?'

'Once or twice. But not much. I told you. He was too lazy to smuggle things. It meant being up all night.'

'He was sometimes up all night drinking.'

'That's different.'

'Were *you* worried?'

'I suppose I was a bit. I mentioned it to his sister, Denise Oudry, but she said he'd always had periods when he'd gone moody. Even as a boy.'

10

That night they decided to go mad and eat at Luigi's in Le Havre du Sud.

Luigi André himself met them with a beaming smile. 'I thought you'd come and see me eventually,' he said. 'I told you this is the best place on the island. That other lot – ' his contempt was enormous ' – they only provide the sort of food tourists eat.' He took the straw hat Pel had brought so he wouldn't drop dead of sunstroke, and hung it up. 'Of course, when I went on about cops on the boat, I didn't know you were one. If I *had* known, I'd have held my tongue. I was talking about the cops on the island. Have you caught our murderer yet?'

'I think you'd have heard if we had,' Pel said dryly.

'That's so.' Luigi laughed. 'Everybody hears everything on this island. Well – ' he paused ' – not *everything*. The cops don't hear much. Not even when there's plenty to hear.'

'Such as what?' Pel asked.

Luigi shrugged. 'We're on the direct route from Italy to Nice, my friend. Via Corsica.'

'What does that mean?'

'Swiss watches, Monsieur. They go into Italy across the lake at Lugano. Very useful that lake. Half of it's Italian. Half of it's Swiss.'

'There's nothing very new in Swiss watches,' Pel pointed out. 'It goes on all the time. Is there something else? Is somebody on the island up to something?'

Luigi shrugged, making a great show of indifference. 'I imagine so, Monsieur.'

'Who? The Vicomte?'

'Why do you suggest the Vicomte?'

'Because he seems to be the only person on the island with enough money to get up to something.'

'There are others, Monsieur.'

'Well, who?'

Luigi's eyes flickered and he drew Pel aside as the others took their seats. 'The people in Nice and Marseilles use us as a stepping stone,' he said quietly.

'For what?'

'Monsieur, I don't know. But there are some unexpected people on this island these days.'

'Such as this type, Rambert, who lives at Muriel?'

'He might be one. He developed Muriel.'

'With his own money?'

'He'd have needed a lot.'

'So where did he get it? The Vicomte?'

Luigi was wary. 'You go on a lot about the Vicomte, Monsieur.'

'*You* go on a lot about mysterious people. I have to make guesses.'

'There were more than the Vicomte in it.'

'But he *was* in it?'

'I think so. I suppose so.'

'What about these others? Who were they?'

'Why do you want to know, Monsieur?'

'Because everything seems to be connected.'

'Even Caceolari's death?'

'Even that.'

'I thought he saw something he shouldn't.'

'Why do you say that?'

'Well, didn't he?'

'Inform me.'

'That's what I heard.'

Pel sniffed. 'That's what *I* heard, too. But if he did see something, what was it? Was he somehow a witness to some sort of shady deal?'

Luigi was wary. 'Who between?'

'Between these people who set up the Muriel project – and perhaps someone else.'

'Who, for instance?'

Pel was losing his temper. 'I'm the one who's asking the questions,' he snapped. 'We're not far from Marseilles and there are a few shady characters there. Come to that, Nice,

91

too. Finally, we're not far from Italy where they have the Mafia. Would anybody like *that* be involved?'

Luigi was beginning to grow nervous. 'Monsieur, I don't know,' he said. 'But some of them got hurt a little while ago you'll remember. Six of them.'

Pel looked up sharply. 'If you know something, you'd better say so,' he said coldly.

Luigi shrugged. 'I know nothing. It doesn't pay to know things. I just guess.'

'*Somebody* had better know something.'

'I expect somebody does.'

'Who, for instance?'

Luigi was looking worried now. 'Doctor Nicolas will always talk for a brandy and soda, I'm told,' he said. 'He's the police doctor so he knows what Beauregard's up to. And he doesn't care what happens to him either. After what happened to him already, why should he?'

'What did happen to him?'

'His wife was in a car accident. Multiple injuries. He put her on morphine to ease her pain and she became an addict. And while she was at it so did his son. They're both dead. It started him on the booze. That's why he came here. Nothing matters much to him any more. He'll tell you, Monsieur.'

Without saying why to Madame or De Troq', Pel decided they should take their after-dinner coffee and brandy by the harbour of the Vieux Port. He was almost enjoying himself – at least he was as near as Pel ever came to that happy state – because it was wonderful to eat and drink what you liked, knowing that no finance committee would query your expenses, better still that they were being paid by someone to whom a million here or there meant nothing.

They found places in the expanse of coloured seats near the harbour that De Troq' had started calling Hell's Half-Acre and as they sat down, Doctor Nicolas appeared alongside them like a spectre – almost as if he'd spotted them and decided they were good for a few drinks. He looked as unwholesome as ever, unshaven – probably even unwashed – his clothes unpressed, his trousers still apparently on the point of dropping round his ankles, his greasy grey hair sticking out from beneath the battered straw hat.

Pel shook hands solemnly and bought him a brandy and soda which he downed at a gulp. His soulful look got him another.

'How long are you staying here on police business?' he asked.

'I'm not here on police business,' Pel said. 'Though you'd never believe it, I'm on my honeymoon.'

Nicolas rose and solemnly removed his hat to Madame Pel. 'My apologies, Madame,' he said. 'I thought you were a police official, too.'

Madame smiled. She seemed flattered.

Pel didn't beat about the bush. 'How well do you know Beauregard?' he asked.

Nicolas held out his hand, palm down, and tilted it from side to side. 'Nobody knows Beauregard,' he said.

'I'm told you know him as well as anybody. After all, you work with him.'

'When I can't avoid it.'

'Does he take bribes?'

Nicolas looked blank. 'How should I know that?'

'I'm told you know a lot of things.'

'Maybe I do. Maybe not. In any case, I mind my own business.'

'I've heard that smuggling goes on round here. Has Beauregard ever caught anybody at it?'

'Not to my knowledge.'

'And that perhaps the gangs in Marseilles have an interest in this place. Luigi said you'd know. Have you heard that?'

Nicolas glanced about him as if he were afraid of being overheard, then he picked up his glass and, holding it in front of his face as if he were about to drink, spoke from behind it.

'Those six who were killed in Nice had been here,' he said quietly.

'How do you know?' Pel was alert at once. 'Did you see them?'

'No.'

'Who did?'

'See Madame Fleurie. Ask about her son. She had one. I brought him into the world.' Nicolas' voice rose nervously and he spoke loudly for everyone in the square to hear. 'The Black Widow. You'll have heard of her, Monsieur. She'll always let you have money. She acts as banker to the whole island. Foreign currency. Bankers' cards. I've often wondered why nobody murders her for what she's got in that safe of hers. I suppose it's because it's so strong nobody can get inside it. But she gives better rates than the hotels. You'll be all right with her.'

'Where does she do business?'

Nicolas gestured with a limp hand towards the narrow streets behind the harbour. 'Down there. You can't miss it. It's an ironmongers' and ship chandlers'.' He laughed. 'It's a joke really. She's a Communist. Eine bisschen Rote. A little Red. I often wonder how much of the money she takes off the capitalist holidaymakers goes to the Communists' fighting fund. Treat her properly, though, because she'll do nothing for you if she takes a dislike to you.'

Nicolas stopped, swallowed the last of his drink and rose abruptly to his feet as if he were anxious to be rid of them. 'Well, I must be on my way,' he said at the top of his voice. 'People dying all over the island. Most of them need a priest, not me, but I have to put in an appearance.'

They watched him shuffling away to the ancient car he drove.

'What was that all about?' Madame Pel said. '*You're* not short of money, are you?'

'No,' Pel said. 'But tomorrow I think I'd better see this Black Widow.'

11

With Madame safely established on the verandah chattering happily to Nelly over coffee, Pel turned his nose in the direction of Madame Fleurie's shop.

'I'll tackle this one myself,' he warned De Troq'. 'Two of us might frighten her off.'

Madame Fleurie's establishment wasn't far from the harbour, down a side street facing an open space where a small bar-restaurant had spread its tables under a flowering acacia. It consisted of a large room that looked like a garage, with two heavy doors painted a rusty red, one of them open to show the interior of an ironmongers' shop. Round the walls were shelves full of tins of paint and emulsion, plastic containers of paraffin and thinners, boxes of brushes, scrapers, trowels, hammers, saws, screwdrivers, vises. In the centre were benches covered with hemp and nylon rope, blocks, tackles, marline spikes, twine, tins of anti-fouling, workmen's gloves. The floor was piled with cartons and boxes of more equipment, rubber boots, rubber gloves, coveralls. The money exchange was behind the closed door and consisted of a desk and nothing else. Standing in a short queue alongside it was a group of newly-arrived holidaymakers. Pel heard both German and English.

Madame Fleurie fitted her nickname. She was dressed entirely in black, a sallow-skinned woman with black eyes like boot buttons circled by purple rings. Her hair was black, going grey, and was dragged back from her face so that she looked like something out of a horror film. Pel could just imagine her showing the heroine into a bedroom to which the vampire had a secret passage.

Studying the tins of paint and emulsion, he waited patiently at the end of the queue as the visitors changed their travellers' cheques and foreign currency. Madame Fleurie was a slow worker and disdained the use of computers, tills or adding machines. She had one drawer in her desk, divided into four compartments, two for French coins and notes, two for foreign coins and notes, and she did all her sums in her head. Behind her, however, stood a large elderly man who looked as though he'd once been a bouncer in a night club, and he seemed to be not only her bodyguard but also her check, because he seemed to count every scrap of money she handled. From time to time people came in for something from the shelves, for screws, nails, twine, a tin of paint, and every time, as the old man served them, Madame Fleurie stopped work until he'd finished. It made changing money a long drawn out business and one or two of the tourists grew tired of waiting and drifted off. 'I'm going to change mine at the hotel,' one of them said. 'I'm wasting good sunbathing hours here.'

The morning dragged and Pel had finally sat down and was half-dozing when he heard Madame Fleurie's voice.

'Monsieur?'

Looking up, he saw the shop was empty and the old bouncer was regarding him suspiciously as if he might have hung on to rob the place. He jumped to his feet.

'Monsieur wishes to change a traveller's cheque?'

'No – '

'Foreign currency?'

Pel shook his head. 'I'm French,' he said.

Madame Fleurie studied him. It was like being studied by a vampire looking for a tender place to sink its teeth in. 'I thought you were Italian,' she said.

Pel was shocked. He had always considered himself the very essence of French good looks. Noble brow. Clear dark eyes – if perhaps a little faded these days and needing spectacles for reading. Soft black hair – thinning a little on top, mind. A Napoleon of sorts even. To be considered to look like an Italian was as bad as being considered to look like an Englishman. While the Italians had too much in the way of features, the English didn't have any at all. They just had eyes, noses and mouths.

The Black Widow was eyeing him speculatively and the old bouncer moved menacingly from behind her chair to the centre of the shop.

'I'm a policeman,' Pel said. 'Chief Inspector. Brigade Criminelle, Police Judiciaire.' He flipped his identity card at them. 'I wish to talk to you.'

Madame Fleurie studied the red, white and blue stripes on the card and looked up. 'About what?'

'About your son.'

'I haven't got a son.'

'Dr. Nicolas said you had.'

'Did he send you?'

'Yes.'

She studied him for a few moments then glanced at the old bouncer. 'Keep an eye on things, Frédéric,' she said.

At that moment a tourist appeared in the doorway, clad in flowered shirt, straw hat and Bermuda shorts. 'Is this where I change my currency?' he asked in halting French.

'No.' Madame Fleurie swept about a hundred thousand francs into a drawer and locked it. 'I've run out of money.' She gestured at the old bouncer. 'Shut the doors, Frédéric. I'm going for lunch.'

As the doors slammed in the tourist's face, she watched until they were locked then gestured at Pel. 'This way, Monsieur.'

Taking out a bunch of keys, she unlocked a door in the wall behind her desk and swept through. Just beyond was a passage and beyond that another door. Unlocking it carefully, she showed Pel into a kitchen. It was little wonder Fleurie had left her. This was obviously the place where she did all her living because there was a television set and armchairs, as shabby as everything else in the old town. The table, like Madame Caceolari's, was covered with an ancient strip of patterned American cloth.

Madame Fleurie gestured at one of the chairs then, turning to a cupboard alongside an enormous safe where she obviously kept all her currency, produced a bottle and glasses.

'Coup de blanc?' she asked.

Pel nodded and she sloshed out the wine.

Sitting down, she looked at Pel. 'Now, Monsieur. What is it you want?'

Pel wasn't sure what he wanted, but, as Luigi André had suggested, Doctor Nicolas had seemed to know everything that went on in the island. Constantly moving about, visiting his patients, a down-at-heel old doctor whom nobody feared,

97

he knew where everybody lived, what they were up to and when they were at home. He was sharper than he looked and had clearly learned a great deal that he shouldn't. Pel decided to try the one clue he'd been given and see what happened.

'Doctor Nicolas said you have a son, Madame.'

She glanced quickly at him, with black eyes that seemed to glow. Then she sipped at her wine and spoke quietly.

'I *had* a son,' she said.

'What happened to him?'

'He was shot.'

'When?'

'Nearly three weeks ago now. In Nice.'

It dawned on Pel what Nicolas had been getting at. 'One of the six in the Bar-Tabac de la Porte?'

'Yes.'

'The one known as La Petite Fleur?' The inference in the name was suddenly obvious. 'Jean Bernard?'

'His name was Jean-Bernard Fleurie.'

'And those others who were shot?' Pel had their names in his head still. 'Richet, Epaulard, Grimeaud, Bayon and Cerbet. They were his friends?'

'They were his associates. My son was a good boy. He never did any harm.'

They never did, Pel thought. Murderers, rapists, torturers were all warmly regarded by their mothers as good boys who never did any harm.

'He was an altar boy,' Madame Fleurie went on. 'He went regularly to church, and to confession. But he grew tired of the island. They all do. He wanted to go to the mainland. He was only nineteen and I asked my husband to stop him. But *he* was involved with the Pinchon woman and never lifted a finger. He got in with a bad lot and they started calling him La Petite Fleur. He was so good-looking. He should never have gone to the mainland. He had a good job here.'

'Working for you?'

'No. He didn't want this.' She gestured. 'He could have been wealthy – ' though there seemed little to show for it, Pel suspected she was one of the richest individuals on the island after the Vicomte ' – but he preferred to work at the château.'

'Doing what?'

'He worked in the packing department. Preparing those

japanned things they get from China and the coffee machines from Sicily. He helped fill the tins and assemble the machines. It made work for a few and a lot of money for one.'

'The Vicomte?'

'Who else?'

He remembered she was a Communist – a strange political view for a woman who seemed to have all the best capitalist instincts. He changed the subject.

'Did Dr. Nicolas know what your son did?'

'Dr. Nicholas knew everything. He brought him into the world. He watched him grow up. He came here sometimes when he had to borrow money. I always lent it to him. He drank so much, you see. But he delivered my son and he liked to talk about him.'

'Did he ever say anything that might indicate why your son's now dead?'

'No.'

'When your son went to the mainland, he got in with Tagliatti's gang, didn't he?'

'He wanted to get married but he couldn't afford to buy a house – the prices have risen so – so he went to Marseilles. He ran errands for Tagliatti, that's all.'

Doubtless involving swindles, blackmail and protection, Pel decided.

'Did he ever come back here?'

'He never forgot to come and see me.' Her smile was proud and wistful and suddenly she was no longer the hard-faced Black Widow who had her finger on the island's currency, just a grieving mother. 'But when they shot him they wouldn't let me bring him home. They said he had to be buried there. Despite the fact that they often came here.'

'Who often came here?'

'My son and his friends.'

'To this island?' This was what Luigi and Doctor Nicolas had been hinting at. 'Did *you* know his friends?'

'Of course.'

'Well?'

'Only by sight.' She gestured through the window at the little restaurant on the corner of the street opposite where Pel could see the disconsolate tourist in Bermuda shorts drowning his sorrows in a glass of beer. 'They sat there. Under the tree.'

'When?'

'The last time they came.'

'When was that?'

'Just before he was – before they were all killed.'

'What were they doing?'

'Talking. They were celebrating.'

'Celebrating what?'

'They were in the money. Jean-Bernard told me. They'd just completed some business.'

'On this island?'

'Something to do with this island, I think.'

'Were they big shots, these friends of his?'

'No. Small fry, really. Jean-Bernard wanted to get close to Tagliatti. But for the time being he was working with these others. Like him, they just ran errands. Collected things.'

'What things?'

She gave him a haggard stare. 'What sort of things *do* they collect? You know that better than I do.'

He acknowledged the fact. Blackmail. Protection payments.

'Jean-Bernard had plenty of money,' she went on. 'New suits. A car. He'd got a nice girl, too. A different one. On the mainland. He showed me her photograph. Madeleine Rou, she was called. Her father was a manufacturer or something in Marseilles. She worked for a night club.'

'Which one?'

'The Kit Kat Club. She was the boss's secretary, Jean-Bernard said. He was proud of her. He was proud of himself. So was Riccio. I saw him slapping him on the back.'

Pel leaned forward 'Riccio? Turidu Riccio, the restaurant proprietor? Did *he* know them?'

'He knew my son.'

'Was *he* with them?'

'Why not?'

'Was he friendly with these gangster friends of your son's?'

'My son wasn't a gangster.'

Pel ignored the comment. 'Was he friendly?' he repeated.

She shrugged. 'They were eating and drinking together.'

'How well did Riccio know your son?'

'When he wasn't at the château, Jean-Bernard worked on his boat. Before he went to Marseilles.'

'And this occasion when they were sitting outside the bar there? When was it? Exactly.'

She shrugged. 'Two weeks before it happened. Before the shooting.'

'Why didn't you tell someone?'

She gave him a hard stare. 'Who? Beauregard?'

He saw her point. 'Well, if not Beauregard, someone else. Why didn't you go to Marseilles and tell the police there?'

'You don't get mixed up with gang feuds.'

'Not even when your son's killed?'

'Not even then.'

'Why didn't you drop a hint in the right place then? Why didn't you see the Vicomte, for instance?'

'No, thank you.'

'Don't you like the Vicomte?'

'There are many reasons why I shouldn't like the Vicomte.'

'Name one. Inform me.'

'He buys votes. He allows the farms on the island to go only to the people who support him. And *they* make sure their tenants and workers do the same. *Anybody* on this island could be removed if he said the word.'

'Why don't you tell someone of this?'

'Who?'

'There's me. I'm listening.'

She studied him for a while. 'He's the enemy of the workers,' she said eventually. 'He puts no money into the soil.'

'Do *you*?'

She looked startled.

'You must have more money than *they* have,' Pel pointed out. 'Do *you* help them?'

'I give my time.'

'So does the Vicomte. If *you* don't give away *your* earnings, why should he?'

'He doesn't live like the workers. I do.'

He had to admit that. The room they were in was among the ugliest and most uncomfortable he'd ever seen, but he wondered if it were because she believed in living like the island's peasants or just because she'd never been educated

101

to anything better. Caceolari had lived in a similar home and so did Magimel and Lesage and everybody else he'd talked to. The islanders didn't exactly go in for a lot of interior decoration.

'Could Riccio have been involved in the shooting of your son?' he asked.

She stirred in her chair. 'My son was his friend. I know they were friends. I *saw* they were friends. Turidu was heart-broken. He came to see me and swore vengeance. He swore he'd find out who did it.'

'And did he?'

'He went to Nice. But he brought nothing back.'

'But when Caceolari was murdered, too, surely you must have wondered what those gangsters were doing here on the island.'

She was silent for a moment before she answered. 'You learn to keep your own counsel. I've told you. *I* learned. What are you going to do?'

'Look into it.'

'Don't mention *I* told you anything. You just came here to get money.'

'They'll think I'm another Beauregard taking bribes.'

'I shall tell them that because of your protracted stay you were short and produced a banker's card. There's nothing illegal about that.'

'Are you afraid of something?'

'This place's too near to Marseilles and Nice. Too near Corsica.'

'They don't go in for vendettas these days.'

'All the same. We're only two hundred kilometres away from Calvi. It's also only a hundred to Bordighera in Italy. Easy trips by boat and there are no customs posts on the sea.'

'What are you getting at, Madame?'

'Nothing.'

Pel rose and reached for his hat.

'Monsieur – ' as she opened the door back into the shop to let him out, she looked up ' – take care of yourself.'

12

Riccio confirmed what Madame Fleurie had said. 'Where did you hear this, Chief?' he asked.

'I heard,' Pel said cautiously. 'I just heard.'

'Well – ' Riccio gestured with the knife with which he was slicing vegetables ' – of course I knew Jean-Bernard. He worked on my boat. In his spare time. Until he went to Marseilles, that is.'

'Did you know he became involved with the gangs in Marseilles?'

Riccio pulled a face. 'I do now. I warned him the last time he came to the island. I got him on one side just before the ferry left. But he was young. He knew it all. He took no notice.'

'Do you remember that occasion? It wasn't long before he was killed. He was sitting in the restaurant opposite his mother's place. With five other men. They were the men who were shot in Nice.'

Riccio frowned. 'Yes, I saw them.'

'You joined them. Drank with them. Did you know they were part of Maurice Tagliatti's gang?'

'I guessed they were part of something. From the way they were dressed. From the way they talked. But what am I supposed to do? I said "Hello" to Jean-Bernard and he pulled out a chair for me. I drank with them. They were in a good mood.'

'Did you know the other five?'

'No. But I soon found out that what I suspected was correct. When I read in the paper that they were all dead. I guessed why.'

'Why?'

'They'd been up to something. They were boasting they'd pulled off a big deal.'

'They didn't say what it was?'

'Smuggling watches or something, I thought. It goes on. But I liked Jean-Bernard, though I thought he was stupid and young. I went to Nice, Monsieur. I swore I'd try to find out who killed him. I made enquiries.'

'That was a highly dangerous thing to do.'

Riccio shrugged. 'I realise that now. I didn't then. I went over there. I asked around.'

'If it had got back to the people who did it, you could have been the next one.'

They left Riccio bent over his charcoal fire and De Troq' grinned.

'Fish again,' he said. 'At least, it smells like fish.'

'It's not the only thing round here that smells of fish,' Pel growled. 'Madame Fleurie seemed to be throwing out strong hints about connections with Corsica and Italy. Let's see if any of the fishing boats ever went there. And do it quietly, too. I have the distinct impression that this island has a lot of ears.'

The following day, De Troq' departed on the ferry for Nice. He was due for a long session with the Prefect of Police there and was going, with help from Marseilles, to Corsica and Italy.

During the afternoon, wanting to know more about the island, Pel searched for a library. But it turned out to consist of one room no bigger than a kitchen – a small kitchen at that – filled with tattered books that looked as if they'd been contributed by nobly-minded people from the stock of those they didn't want on their own shelves. A few youngsters sat at tables alongside dozing old men who were pretending to read. Pel didn't even bother to go past the door.

He was shocked. A chauvinist if ever there were one, he had never had any doubt that France was the most cultured nation in the world – with Burgundy as its focal spot, and the village where Evariste Clovis Désiré Pel had been born the very heart of that spot – and that such a country shouldn't have a library within reach of every one of its citizens was an appalling indication of neglect. The Vicomte had a lot to answer for, he decided. Perhaps even, he thought, it was deliberate. His activities on the island called for an intelligent opposition but there was none at all and perhaps that was how he liked to keep it.

'Monsieur would like to borrow a book or two perhaps?' Nelly asked. 'I have many James Bonds and a biography of Sophia Loren. I've even got *War and Peace*. I bought it when I saw the film but I've never read it.'

'Has anyone?' Pel asked. 'I was wanting an encyclopaedia, as a matter of fact.'

On Nelly's suggestion he telephoned the château and asked if he might use the library there.

'Just an encyclopaedia,' he explained.

It was Tissandi who answered. The Vicomte, he said, was in Paris, having crossed by launch to the mainland and taken a flight to the capital.

'Business, of course,' he said. 'He has many interests, you understand, and a daughter who lives there. But, of course, he'd be more than pleased to have you visit the château. Why not bring Madame to tea? I'll be happy to show you round the place.'

Madame was delighted but she wasn't in the slightest deluded. 'You couldn't care less about the island,' she pointed out. 'You have other ideas, haven't you?'

Pel shrugged. 'Geneviève de mon coeur,' he said, 'I can see I'm going to be able to hide nothing from you.'

They didn't even have to drive up to the château. The Vicomte's personal Citroën was sent down for them and, sunk deep in its cushions, they were whirled in silence and comfort up the hill. Ignazi and Tissandi met them at the door. The sun was hot and they were glad to be in the cooler atmosphere of the château. Shown at once to the library, Ignazi indicated a vast encyclopaedia laid out, volume by volume, on a long oak table. All they had to do was turn the pages. None of your hoisting down of heavy volumes. That had all been done for them.

'We'll leave you here, Chief Inspector,' Tissandi explained. 'When you've done your research, pull the bell and we'll take tea together.'

As they disappeared, Pel closed the door after them and stared round him. The library was situated in the round tower on the end of the château and comprised three circular floors like shelves so that it was possible to look down from the top to the ground floor. Above them was the turret, a magnificent affair of vast oak beams.

Madame looked at Pel, anxious to be of help.

'Turn up St. Yves,' he suggested.

As she did so, he moved further along and, searching for the letter 'I', began to turn to Italy. Madame looked puzzled. 'What am I looking for?' she asked.

'The island. They say it dates back to Roman times. Tiberius had a villa here, didn't he?'

'That was Capri.'

'Then it must have been Julius Caesar. They also say that Georges Sand and Chopin came here once and that's why they decided to take that winter in Majorca when it rained all the time and ruined the piano.'

Pel's search seemed to cover a lot of ground and not much of it seemed to concern the island, but Madame was already learning, as his squad back home had long since learned, that when Pel was on a scent his mind worked in weird and wonderful ways and he was best left alone. She'd been given the task of reading about the island merely to give her something to do, so she idly turned the pages and looked at the pictures, and left him to it.

When he'd finished what he was doing, he pulled the bell. Tissandi must have been waiting on the edge of his chair down the corridor because he arrived within seconds.

'Let's go to the terrasse,' he said.

The terrasse, different from the one where Pel had sat taking apéritifs with the Vicomte on his first visit, looked over the harbour of the Vieux Port. Below them through the trees they could see the russet tiles of the old houses. It was the hottest part of the day and coloured umbrellas had been erected to keep the sun off them. As the tray of tea arrived, Tissandi produced a bottle of champagne.

'More interesting than tea,' he smiled.

'Do you produce wine here?' Madame asked.

'Of course. Let me present you with some. The Vicomte would approve, I'm sure.' Ringing the bell, Tissandi murmured to the manservant who appeared. 'We have the perfect place for the vines,' he explained as the footman vanished. 'Slatey slopes facing south.'

When the manservant reappeared he was carrying a carton.

106

'Château Rochemare,' Tissandi said. 'Make sure it's uncorked long enough and you'll have a splendid wine for your main course.'

He whispered to the manservant and turned to Pel. 'It'll be waiting for you when you leave.'

When they'd finished the champagne and cakes, Tissandi suggested they might like to see the freezers. Climbing into the Citroën, they were driven across the estate to what had once been the stables. Inside were vast freezing plants. Several women were moving about, one or two of them with children.

'They come from the villages,' Tissandi explained. 'The Vicomte takes an interest in everything, even his workers.'

Especially his *female* workers, Pel thought.

Behind the stables there were vast warehouses, filled with cartons.

'Raisins,' Tissandi explained. 'Dried grapes.'

In another of the buildings men and women were putting together the red Rapido coffee machines. Nearby, other smaller machines were being assembled.

'Rapido Miniatures,' Tissandi explained. 'They've become tremendously popular in the last year or two. We import them from Italy as kits and assemble them here. It reduces the import duties and increases the profits. The Vicomte's a very good businessman. We get them from Calvi.'

'*Who* gets them from Calvi?'

Tissandi turned. 'Well, sometimes I go over there and make the arrangements. Sometimes it's Freddy Ignazi here. If the Vicomte fancies a holiday, he goes himself. He takes his boat across. You'll have seen his launch – we all enjoy it – and he has a house near the harbour there. He can do the journey in a few hours and, of course, he always chooses a calm day. When your time's your own, why make yourself miserable?'

In another part of the stables, there were more cartons and the japanned boxes that Madame Fleurie had mentioned standing on the table. 'From Taiwan,' Tissandi explained. 'They contain tea. They're popular because they're so attractive.' His fingers ran over the fire-breathing dragons on the outside. 'Traditional Chinese dragons, of course. We have an agent in Hong Kong who imports them and ships them here. We're the agents for the southern half of France.'

Pel ran his finger round the edge of one of the boxes. The lid had been heavily waxed.

'To keep the flavour in, of course,' Tissandi explained. 'China tea is much more delicate than Indian tea.'

They left in the Range Rover, the case of wine in the rear, and were driven in style down the hill to the Duponts' house. Standing on the verandah with the case of wine in his arms, Pel watched the car drive away, then placing the case on the kitchen table, he took out his notebook.

'Corsica,' he said, reading what he'd written. 'Chief exports: wool, wood, wheat, wine, cork, tobacco, silk-worms, oranges. Switzerland – via Italy, of course – watches, optical and scientific instruments. Italy: cheap typewriters, radios, televisions, bicycles.'

'*And* coffee making machines,' Madame Pel pointed out.

'And coffee making machines,' Pel agreed. 'Now, apart from the coffee making machines which we know about, which of those articles are coming through St. Yves into France?'

'Is that what you think those people who were killed were up to? Smuggling?'

Pel shook his head. 'Not really,' he admitted. 'They don't seem to have been important enough. There was somebody bigger than them behind it. Tagliatti? I doubt it.'

He frowned. Tagliatti was a smooth young man who wore suits of a type Pel could never afford to wear, drove Mercedes and Rolls-Royce cars, and was surrounded by a bevy of girls who looked as if they had been borrowed from the French and Italian film industries.

'All the same,' he said aloud, 'he's just the sort, if it were worth it.'

13

The house of Lesage, the garage owner, lay behind the Vieux Port, where the road climbed from the town and began to curl into the hills. As the telephone bell rang, Lesage sat bolt upright in bed, his ferret face alert, his wife alongside him, awake as fast as he was, also on the alert. They came to consciousness quickly because they were used to being awakened.

As Lesage reached for the telephone his wife hurried downstairs and a moment later her husband shouted after her. 'Call the boys out!' he yelled.

Half-dressed in parts of a seedy uniform, he flung himself out of the house to his car and by the time he had reached the town, several other members of the island's little fire brigade were edging out the fire engine. It wasn't a very modern fire engine. It dated back to World War II and had actually done service in Marseilles when that city had been in danger of bombing. Sold eventually, when no one else wanted it, it had finally been refurbished and re-engined and had found its way to St. Yves. It still wasn't a very good apparatus but there wasn't much for it to do on St. Yves – at least not until recently when the cases of arson had appeared among the holiday homes – and there wasn't a single house on the island more than two storeys, save the hotel in the Vieux Port which was fitted with a fire alarm system and had staff drilled to handle emergencies. Moreover, its crew knew that if a fire grew too big for them they could always rely for support on the Vicomte de la Rochemare's own private apparatus, which was kept in one of the stables behind the château in case of fire there and had occasionally been called out when brush fires had broken out on the dry hillsides in summer.

As they scrambled aboard, someone tugged at the bell. The

electric bell had long since given up the ghost and they had to use a hand bell, which was operated by a cord attached to the windscreen. As the machine gathered speed, a car appeared, drew up among the other cars hurriedly parked on the patch of bare earth alongside the fire station by their owners, the fire engine's crew, and its driver scrambled out carrying his uniform, and was heaved aboard the fire engine.

As they hurtled along the harbour front, the engine roaring, the equipment clattering, the bell ringing in sporadic bursts, the noise was enough to disturb Pel. He listened for a moment, assuming that the island's arsonist had been at work again, and went back to sleep.

The following morning he learned that Doctor Nicolas was dead.

Babin, the postman, brought the news and it seemed to have shocked him. 'It went up like a bomb,' he said.

Pel was shocked, too. He'd taken a curious liking to the old doctor, scruffy as he was.

'Another one for Billy the Burner?'

Babin was white. 'No, no! Not this time! After all, Doc Nicolas *lived* here. He'd been here for fifteen years or so. Besides, I reckon it must have been petrol. All the others were paraffin.'

'They were?'

'So Beauregard said. Everybody knew about it.'

'How did you find out?'

'I was up there delivering letters. I don't know who gave the alarm. But whoever it was, it was too late. The place was well alight.'

'I think,' Pel said, 'that I'd better go and have a look.'

Doctor Nicolas's house was little more than a heap of charred timbers inside a square of scorched, blackened and half-fallen walls. There was an ancient van there doing duty for an ambulance and the island fire brigade, collecting their gear to depart, looked dirty, stained with water and utterly baffled. On the path was the scorched and saturated body of a ginger cat.

There were a few people from the nearby houses watching what was going on. Among them was Luz Robles. Her face was stiff and her make-up smudged, and her hair was loosely tied in a coil.

'It's Doctor Nicolas,' she said in a shocked voice.

'Yes.'

'Why him? He was a good man.'

'Did you see what happened?'

'No. The noise of people shouting wakened me.'

'You saw no one?'

'No one at all except the fire brigade.'

A grimy figure appeared alongside them. Through his mask of caked sweat and soot, Pel recognised Lesage, the garage proprietor.

'We hadn't a chance,' he said. 'It was going up like a furnace. *He* didn't have a chance either. They're trying to get him out now. We've found him. He was in bed. He's not much burned. Suffocated on the smoke, I reckon. I suppose he'd had one too many brandies.'

'He'd been smoking in bed?'

'No sign of it. But there was a hell of a fire going. It started near the bottom of the stairs. He had two or three cane chairs there that he used outside in the hot weather. They were burned out.'

'So how did it happen?'

'Well, it wasn't Billy the Burner.' Lesage's view was the same as the postman's. 'It's different. *He* sprinkles paraffin about and he always does his stuff when the place's unoccupied. Besides he'd never do it to Doc Nicolas. Not if he was an islander, which he must be. This one's different.'

'How different? Inform me.'

Lesage wiped some of the grime off his face. 'We found a window undone,' he said. 'But that's not unusual. People don't lock their houses here when they're in them and besides – ' he gestured with his head at the body of the cat ' – he had that old cat of his, Minou. He was fond of it and always left a window open for it to go in and out. Somebody saw that open window and used it. It's near the bottom of the stairs close to where those cane chairs were. If you ask me, someone tossed something in and chucked a match after it. If he'd had one or two drinks, he wouldn't know a thing about it. The place would be full of smoke and the staircase would be like a funnel full of flames in minutes.'

111

'Couldn't he have jumped out?'

'He might have if he'd been sober. But most evenings he wasn't. If there were an emergency – a baby or something – they always had to send me and the wife to make strong black coffee to bring him round.'

The ambulance men – like the firemen all volunteers and amateurs – appeared, carrying a stretcher containing a long narrow shape covered with a blanket.

'Old Doc was all right,' Lesage said. 'He was a good doctor. And as often as not he forgot to charge people for his visits.'

'So why set his house on fire?'

'God knows. If it *was* this type who's doing it round the island, he's gone too far this time.'

Yes, Pel thought. If it *were* the type who was doing it round the island. But this time, like Lesage, he had a feeling it wasn't.

Doctor Nicolas had been a shadowy character, keeping to himself, with no friends beyond his old cat. Nobody had seen him speaking to anyone after he had seen Pel. Indeed, no one had noticed him at all because he had a cobwebby sort of manner of moving about, quiet, shadowy, alone, and seemed to have a habit of disappearing into the wallpaper.

Madame Fleurie had heard, though. 'He's dead, isn't he?' she asked.

'Yes, he is.'

She showed no emotion. 'He was a good man. Somebody killed him.'

'That seems to be the case,' Pel agreed. 'Would you know who might wish to?'

She shrugged. 'Doctor Nicolas knew everything that went on, on the island. He was always moving about. He knew every family.'

Riccio had also heard. 'Think someone saw you talking to me about those types with Jean-Bernard, Chief?' he demanded.

'Why do you ask?'

'Well, if someone did, he probably thought Doctor Nicolas had put you up to it. He did, didn't he? That was why you asked.'

There was no point in denying. 'Yes,' Pel agreed. 'Indirectly he did.'

'That's why he was killed.' Riccio slapped his forehead with the heel of his hand. 'If you need help, Chief, ask for me. I'll do what I can. I liked old Nicolas.'

It seemed to indicate another visit to the château. The Vicomte was still on the mainland but Tissandi promised to attend to all the details of the burial.

'No point in looking for relations,' he said. 'Because he hadn't got any. The only ones we knew about were his wife and son and they're dead. Still – ' he shrugged ' – there's not much to interest anyone. He hadn't any money. He hadn't any possessions. Just a few sticks of furniture, an old car, that cat and what he stood up in. Even the house wasn't his. We let him have it. For nothing.'

When Pel reached the Duponts' house, Lesage was waiting for him. He had formed an opinion about the cause of the fire. 'Weed killer, sugar and acid,' he said. 'Put that lot together and there's an instantaneous and violent outbreak. We've found the bottle. We're still clearing up. The acid eats through the cork and flows through on to the other mixture. When that happens there are flames.'

'Who'd know how to do it?'

Lesage shook his head. 'Don't ask me. It's not hard to find out these things these days. Kids learn them at school. They learn them from the television. I don't tell them. I didn't tell you but I expect you know them, too.'

'I know them.'

'I'll let you have the bottle. I expect you'll want it. To send to the forensic people.'

'Yes,' Pel agreed. 'I shall want it. But I doubt if it will tell us anything.'

Lesage shook his head. 'Somebody had it in for Old Doc. Perhaps someone he once gave evidence against. When he was a police surgeon. They tried to make it look like one of Billy the Burner's jobs. But it wasn't the same. We knew that from the start.'

With Doctor Nicolas dead, there was nobody to give any opinions on exactly what had killed him. Arrangements were made for a police surgeon to come from the mainland but it wasn't desperately necessary. Somebody, for some reason, had taken an objection to the old man and killed him by setting his house on fire so that he'd suffocated on the smoke when he'd had one too many brandies and sodas.

But why?

Had someone seen the old man talking to Pel and guessed at the hints he'd dropped? It seemed more than likely. So who was it? Hell's Half-Acre was big enough with enough small bars round it to hide the whole of Tagliatti's gang, if need be. Had someone been watching and seen Doctor Nicolas' little performance when he'd advised Pel to see Madame Fleurie? It could have been anyone on the island, and Madame Fleurie was clearly wise to mind her own business.

So who knew Doc Nicolas' habits? To whom had he spoken after seeing Pel? Who were his friends? It had to be one of his friends because the consensus of opinion was that he'd had no enemies. But neither, so they claimed, had Caceolari, who'd been too lazy to make them. The only conclusion that could be reached, therefore, was that Nicolas had been murdered for much the same reason as Caceolari. Because he knew something.

14

Feeling they needed to get away from the depressing facts of Doctor Nicolas' death, Pel took his wife back to Luigi's at Le Havre du Sud. Anything was better than Riccio's swordfish and Luigi's food *was* as good as he claimed.

As the waiter took Madame's coat, Luigi drew Pel to one side again. He had heard of Doctor Nicolas' death and, like Riccio, was quick to assume it was because he'd been seen talking to Pel.

'It's my fault,' he said in grieving tones. 'I put you on to him.'

'Nobody knew that but you,' Pel pointed out acridly.

Apéritifs appeared quickly – almost, Pel thought, as a sop to Luigi's conscience – and because Pel was never in favour of cool night air, they ate inside rather than among a group of tourists from Denmark who were outside under the coloured lights. Because it was something they were rarely able to do in their own country, sitting outside – despite the fact that their food congealed at great speed – made them feel they were really on holiday.

They ate fish followed by veal in cream and drank a bottle of house wine which was rough but good. For a long time they sat in silence then Madame touched Pel's hand.

'You know, Pel,' she said. 'I think you're actually enjoying yourself.'

Pel gave her a sombre look. 'It's a good meal,' he said.

'I don't mean that. I mean you're enjoying what's happening.'

'With Doctor Nicolas dead?'

She pulled a face. 'I didn't mean that either, of course. I mean because you're busy. I don't think you'd enjoy merely being on holiday and sitting in the sun.'

Pel admitted the fact. He was the worst sightseer and sitter in the sun in the world. He normally had enough energy for half a dozen – except between waking and drinking his first cup of coffee and smoking his first cigarette. Even to the point of needing less sleep than most people, something which had often been a problem because he'd always been convinced he couldn't sleep, when the real trouble was that he went to bed too early. In the days of Madame Routy early nights had seemed to be important but now he was married they no longer seemed so and he could only assume he'd been bored. As for seeing sights, he could think of nothing more dull.

'Aren't *you* bored?' he asked. 'All day on your own.'

'Oh, I'm all right,' Madame said. 'Nelly and I prepare the meals together then we go out for the day in the Duponts' Renault – it always pleases me that it's theirs because I keep thinking how they tried to swindle us over the Villa des Roses.'

Pel managed a smile. 'The Vicomte has his own ways of dealing with people.'

'Exactly. So we drive to the harbour and have coffee in the sun there. At first Nelly was a little dubious but I told her I wanted her to come with me. She shows me where to go on the island. We went to a church on a cliff yesterday. Near L'Aride. Just big enough to hold a dozen people. Built for a tiny community that used to live there. It overlooks a sheer drop of five hundred feet into the sea. You should let me take you. It's time you had a day or two off.'

'I think I'm going to be too busy.'

'Well, *one* day then. Tomorrow.'

With some reluctance, Pel agreed. 'Just one,' he agreed. 'While De Troq's away.' He ordered another carafe of wine and explained. 'He's bringing back a couple of cops from the mainland.'

Her eyes lit up. 'Are you going to arrest someone?'

'Not immediately. But he's bringing help and he has instructions to arrange that the men he brings will be relieved at the end of a fortnight with, at the end of another fortnight, another group to relieve *them*.'

Madame looked startled. 'Are we likely to be here that long?'

'Are you worried about your business?'

'Oh, no.' She beamed at him. 'That will be quite safe. I

can use the telephone to check up on things. I'm quite enjoying myself as a matter of fact.'

'When will your sister be here?'

'She won't. She telephoned to say she's ill. I'm quite happy.' Madame touched Pel's hand and beamed at him. 'I'm far too busy to want her here, anyway. She always talks about her illnesses and goes to church all the time. And she doesn't drink because she considers it not only sinful but bad for you. I only thought of her because I thought I might be bored. But I'm not. Nelly's an excellent companion. So good, in fact, I thought of asking her to come and work for me.'

'Instead of Madame Routy?' Pel asked hopefully.

'No. In my business. But she's getting married next year. To a man who runs an estate agency near St. Trop'.'

They ate breakfast in the sunshine, with good strong coffee of the sort that Madame Routy had never managed to produce and fresh croissants fetched by Nelly from the bakery near the church. She also brought back a newspaper, a day old but enough to read over breakfast. The shootings in Marseilles had disappeared beneath all the other murders, rapes and butcheries, the scandals and the oppressions in foreign countries that filled the pages. It was a sick sort of world when you considered it. Pel had always believed this but, on holiday, he had to admit, it was inclined to look different and much further away.

Dressing leisurely, he allowed his wife to drive him to the church she'd found, but refused to stand at the rail at the cliff edge.

'Come close, Pel,' she said. 'The view's breathtaking.'

Pel stayed firmly where he was. Breathtaking views, he'd always found, meant a sheer drop and sheer drops made his stomach churn.

They found a farmhouse in the hills where they ate lunch. There was nothing very special about it – the hors d'oeuvres looked like hors d'oeuvres, the meat was meat-coloured; all that was lacking was the flavour – but there was an excellent local wine and it cost so little Pel was prepared to forget about the taste. Apparently, the farm often had walkers up from the Vieux Port – Britons, usually, who were mad enough to want to climb into the hills during the heat of the summer and, having arrived there, breathless, lost and almost in a state of collapse, promptly started demanding refreshments. The farmer's wife had turned it into a useful business by always encouraging them to stay for lunch which she served in the garden among the flowers. The fact that her customers were usually English, Pel decided, probably accounted for the indifferent cuisine because every Frenchman knew that the English lived on fish and chips, or roast meat and soggy vegetables.

Afterwards, they drove back towards the harbour and, leaving the car under the trees, walked along the rocks. There were several private gardens, all liberally plastered with notices to keep inquisitive holidaymakers out. One, obviously intended for the invading British, read *Entry is forbiten. Violaters will be denounced.*

As they turned away, Pel found himself staring down at a dozen figures enjoying the hot sun on a small beach. Among them, a man was rubbing sun tan oil on himself. He was as bald as an egg and his body was the colour of old mahogany. Then, as he moved, Pel saw that he was stark naked and it dawned on him that everyone else on the beach, women and children, were stark naked too.

Grasping Madame's hand, he turned her briskly round and headed back for the car. While it didn't worry him to see other people naked, he knew that the unwritten rule about nudist beaches was that they didn't allow people on them wearing clothes, and the thought of himself without his clothes standing in the full searchlight glare of the sun was enough to put him completely off his stroke.

De Troq' arrived back on the afternoon ferry with forensic information on the bullets taken from the bodies in the Bar-Tabac de la Porte.

'They thought we might like to have it,' he said, tapping his briefcase. 'Photographs and everything. The ballistic boys say they were killed by 9mm bullets fired, they think, from a British Sterling or Patchett sub-machine gun. Common among British Nato forces. A few have found their way underground. They think this was one. Probably came south from Germany.'

Taking De Troq' to one of the harbour bars, Pel found

seats in the centre of the half-acre of plastic chairs so that they couldn't be overheard, and ordered drinks. De Troq' nodded to three young men in jeans and striped shirts a few tables away.

'Claverie, Lebrun and Mangin,' he said quietly. 'Detective sergeants. They stay for a fortnight as holidaymakers, then they're relieved by three more, Ledoyer, Berthelot and Morel. They hope we'll have sorted it all out by then. They're staying at a hotel in Le Havre du Sud. We can contact them by telephone. It only requires a word and they'll meet us here and we can get into conversation, accidentally-on-purpose. They've brought a radio we can use to contact Nice at any time.'

A certain Inspector Maillet was handling the case on the mainland. Nice didn't consider the affairs of a small island warranted one of their senior officers, all of whom were involved with affairs of their own because, with six murders on their hands and being so close to Marseilles, Nice wasn't exactly noted as a city of lilywhite morals.

'He's also watching the wives and girl friends of the dead men.' De Troq' smiled. 'Because they noticed that Tagliatti's boys are watching them, too. So Maillet's wondering if those six who were shot stashed away some loot somewhere first. Was that why they were shot, in fact?'

'And if so, who's got it now?'

'Exactly. When they find out, there'll be a rush between the cops and Tagliatti's mob to get there first.'

'What about Italy? Have any fishing boats from St. Yves been seen in Italian ports?'

De Troq' smiled. 'Yes,' he said and, as Pel sat up, interested, he went on. 'All of them.'

'Their identification numbers,' he continued, 'are prefixed by IY – Ile de St. Yves – and the coastguards and harbourmasters always make a note of visiting boats. We did a check and they've *all* been spotted at one time or another. Chiefly they go to Bordighera – because it's closest, I suppose – but everything always seems to be above board. They buy cartons of food because it's cheaper in Italy than it is in France and they appear to be on ordinary fishing trips. But that's fairly normal. Everybody does it and they didn't exceed the allowance. That's all there is to it.'

'And Corsica?'

'They've been seen in Calvi, too.'

Pel lit a cigarette. He had fought them off all day but now, with De Troq's information, they were rushing at him again, demanding to be smoked. He shook out the match guiltily, noticing that De Troq's eyes were on him.

'Calvi to Bordighera,' he mused. 'Bordighera to the Ile de St. Yves. The Ile de St. Yves to Marseilles. Marseilles to the rest of France. It makes sense.'

De Troq' smiled. 'There's more, Patron,' he said.

'Inform me.'

De Troq' had also brought back a thick sheaf of papers on the enquiry into the affairs of the Bureau of Environmental Surveys. The Government, it seemed, had long since noticed that the Ministry of Beaux Arts was getting itself involved in a surprising number of shady deals. Nobody suspected the Ministry of Beaux Arts, of course, but it appeared that quite a lot of people were making money from development projects when they shouldn't have been and there was a great deal of suspicion centred on the Bureau of Environmental Surveys, and suddenly particularly on the deputy minister, Jean-Jacques Hardy, who had been watched for some time and was at that moment appearing before a sub-committee of the House of Representatives to give evidence against the Minister.

'Why have you brought this back?' Pel asked. 'We're not investigating Hardy.'

'We might be, Patron,' De Troq' said. 'You remember we asked them to make enquiries about Rambert's friends. Well, it seems Hardy might have been one. He had a house at Muriel. He sold it last year.'

Pel leaned forward. 'Tell me more. If he had a house here what we're investigating might *well* be part of his set-up.'

De Troq' sank half his beer and smiled. 'The fraud squad have been watching him closely,' he said. 'And it's been noticed that his life style's changed a lot in the last two years. He's not inherited money and his wife has none so they're wondering how it is he can start investing in property. None of his Ministry's property's involved, but it's property nevertheless. He seems above board but anybody with money to throw around's under suspicion, and it's been noticed that *he's* been doing just that. He has a woman in the 6th. District of Paris. She's got a title and – ' De Troq' smiled ' – people with titles have expensive tastes, Patron. I know. I'm one. He's also just bought a large new car and, as well as a flat in Meudon, he has a yacht at Ste. Marguerite which he bought from a financier called Addou. He didn't get those out of his salary.'

He flicked over the pages of his notebook. 'He's careful, of course,' he went on. 'And he seems to move about between his contacts with caution. He never seems to be with the same one twice, and let's face it, the people he meets in the street and talks to could be merely acquaintances. Recently, though, he's been seeing a tall chap who's a bit of a dandy. They're not sure what they can pin on him. They know he was in financial difficulties a few years ago but he's now safely out of them and he claims he sorted himself out by means of a loan from an American called Elliott. They've seen Elliott, who's agreed he lent the money but he was unable to produce any evidence in the form of a receipt or any notations in his bank account to prove it. It seems *he* has a somewhat shady reputation, too. Hardy's now claiming to be a sick man and his doctors are producing proof that he shouldn't be giving evidence to the enquiry. It's a dodge to avoid answering questions, of course, because the fraud boys have a feeling they've got him. Some of his money has *also* been used to buy shares in a big plate glass combine that's just gone public. It was owned by a man called Kern who stands to make a pile from the sale, while Hardy stands to pick up a bit from the shares. It's where he got the money he used to buy them that puzzles everybody.'

'It's a pretty tenuous link with our case,' Pel said.

'Not as tenuous as you might think, Patron. Because Tagliatti owned shares in that company, too.'

'Did he indeed?' Pel was silent for a moment then he stubbed out his cigarette. 'And Tagliatti? Where's he?'

de Troq' smiled. 'Still out of the way in Switzerland,' he said.

15

The case had begun to take on a new perspective. If Hardy and Tagliatti – especially Tagliatti – had interests on St. Yves, then Caceolari's death might have been due to something that had nothing at all to do with smuggling. Yet it was clear he'd seen *something* and surely Hardy and Tagliatti wouldn't have been conducting any of their shifty financial deals down at the harbour on a moonlit night. Especially since Tagliatti had been in Switzerland at the time and Hardy was in Paris giving evidence to the committee of enquiry. Perhaps Caceolari had no connection with their affairs whatsoever.

So what had he seen? They knew he'd talked to someone about it, though they didn't know whom, and, apart from the talk with his wife when he'd said he'd seen Riccio's boat returning from his fishing trip, he seemed to have said little else.

At least to his wife.

But he had seen something. And it had ended up with him being murdered. So whom had he told about it? He must have told *someone*, because that was surely the reason why he was dead. The word had surely got back that he'd seen something illegal and his mouth had been shut – for good.

'By Riccio, Patron?' De Troq' asked. 'Could it have been him?'

Pel considered. 'It was Riccio's boat he saw that night,' he said thoughtfully. 'And Caceolari was obviously afraid of him. Why? Was Riccio involved in this smuggling everybody seems to talk about?'

'It's not far to Italy, Patron.'

'No.' Pel frowned. 'But it couldn't have been *smuggling* that worried Caceolari. He'd done a bit himself. That wouldn't upset him. It was seeing that boat.'

De Troq' didn't interrupt Pel's train of thought and he went on slowly.

'There was something on that boat that worried him. Riccio said he'd been fishing – and he might well have been – but there was something else he brought back that Caceolari saw. What?'

'Or *who*, Patron?'

Pel acknowledged the possibility. 'Or *who*? People? Illegal immigrants? Italians trying to get into France? It's not unknown.'

De Troq' gestured. 'He told his wife he *saw* them bringing fish ashore. A good catch, he said – which was also what Riccio said – and we know that it was heavy and they carried it ashore in a tarpaulin – '

'Why not in baskets?'

De Troq's head lifted. 'Baskets?'

'You don't usually carry fish in tarpaulins. You carry them in baskets.'

'You think it might *not* have been fish, Patron?'

'It's a possibility.'

'One of these illegal immigrants?'

'That's also a possibility?'

'Dead?'

'It has been known. There have been rackets where money's been accepted to smuggle people in and then they've been found dead. Saves time and trouble.'

'You think it was somebody *they*'d killed?'

'Well, we know Riccio was there. And Maquin the cooper. Caceolari said so.'

He had indeed – to his wife – but, whatever it was he saw, it seemed that for a week at least, from the night he saw it until the night Pel had arrived on the island, he had been sufficiently reassured that there was nothing to worry about to have gone about his normal business in roughly his normal manner. Which seemed to suggest that, if he saw anything, it wasn't a body; because surely that would have frightened him enough to go to the police at once.

But why in the end hadn't the reassurance been enough and why had the sight of Riccio leaning against the wall of the bar when he'd arrived to collect Pel and his wife from the ferry been enough to start up his fears all over again? Since

123

he was dead within a matter of hours, it seemed he'd had good reason to be afraid. Riccio's presence at the harbour had been an implied threat. He must have been watching for some time where Caceolari went and had obviously followed him about the island. And Caceolari in the end had *known* he was being followed and had worried about it on and off from the moment he'd realised. Under the circumstances, it wasn't surprising that he'd rushed to see Pel. But why? Why had Riccio's presence frightened him? Why Riccio?

Doubtless there'd been threats. Perhaps Caceolari had hoped to tell his fears to the Vicomte but, finding him on one of his trips away from the island, had told them to someone else instead. But, if that was so, why hadn't that other person done more to protect Caceolari? There seemed to be a great many ramifications to the affair, all of them seemingly involved with corruption and double dealing, and instead of receiving the protection he'd expected, Caceolari had seen only the implied threat of Riccio leaning against the wall of the bar. And *why* was Riccio a menace? Had *he* been up to something shady? And if so, *how* had he learned that Caceolari had seen him?

'The Robles woman, Patron?'

Pel frowned. 'It seems unlikely. They were an odd mixture but I got the impression that she actually liked him.'

De Troq' stared at the table. 'Beauregard?' he said. 'He probably went to see Beauregard and told *him* what he thought.'

It was a possibility.

'It would explain what happened to Doc Nicolas,' Pel said thoughtfully. 'Nicolas knew that Jean-Bernard Fleurie was a runner for Tagliatti's gang. He'd watched him grow up and become a man and saw him go wrong. And he'd been a police surgeon in Marseilles so he probably recognised one or more of the others. The older ones, perhaps, whom he'd remember.The one they called The Chinese, perhaps. Or the man they called Mick the Brick. It seems very possible. And having seen them with young Fleurie, like Caceolari he must have put two and two together and guessed what Jean-Bernard was up to.'

Cautiously they questioned Beauregard but the brigadier said that though Caceolari had often talked to him – they'd often been together in the Place du Port because of their different jobs – he had said nothing to him about anything that might have worried him.

They didn't mention their suspicions, half hoping Beauregard might let something drop that would indicate he knew what they were after, but he was either very careful or he really didn't know. And none of his constables had mentioned anything. They could only assume that Caceolari had told nobody anything beyond the mysterious individual Lesage thought he'd been to see.

Since Beauregard couldn't – or wouldn't – help them, they tried Madame Caceolari again. But she was as vague as before, as were Caceolari's friends, Lesage, Magimel, Rolland and Desplanques.

They also asked among the people Caceolari knew in the Vieux Port, Biz and Le Havre du Sud. Warily, though, giving nothing away, causing no alarm. But nobody knew a thing, and nobody else had noticed the boat Caceolari said he'd seen. Since it had been in the early hours of the morning, it wasn't surprising.

As a last restort they telephoned the château. The Vicomte was still on his jaunt out of the island. 'He's in Calvi.' Ignazi answered Pel's question cheerfully. 'On business. Flew from Marseilles. He has a house there, as you probably know. He would never stay in a hotel.'

'Suppose he went to India?' Pel said coldly. 'He'd have to stay in a hotel then.'

'Not on your life. He knows people all over the world. He'd get someone to lend him or rent him an apartment. And it'd be a good one, too. You can bet on that.'

Obtaining the Vicomte's telephone number, Pel returned to Beauregard's office. It was going to be a long call going a long way and it was going to cost the Vicomte something. But Rochemare greeted him warmly and agreed to answer any questions he wished to ask.

Pel got down to the job at once. 'The taxi-driver, Caceolari,' he said.

'We used him on a temporary basis, occasionally,' Rochemare admitted. 'I believe Tissandi represented me at the funeral. I'm often invited to funerals. Weddings, too.

Sometimes even to christenings. I'm regularly asked to be godfather. It costs me money, I have to admit.'

Probably with reason, Pel thought. Especially if the children happened to be the Vicomte's own. Since he had so much control over everybody's lives on the island, it was just possible that he also had control of the droits de seigneur, too.

'Caceolari was worried,' he said.

'So I understand.'

'He wanted to see somebody to talk about it. Did he see you?'

'No. I'm quite sure about that. I was away from the island from the 13th. – that was the night when the murders in Nice took place – until the end of the week. And all that week-end – the 21st. – I had guests.'

'Who, Monsieur?'

'Paul de Mor and his wife and family. That's Baron de Mor, of course, you understand.'

'Of course.' Pel answered gravely as if he had known Paul, Baron de Mor, since childhood.

'They're old friends. They returned to the mainland the day before the storm. The day before you arrived. The day before Caceolari was murdered.'

'That still left the whole day, Monsieur.'

'He didn't come and see me. I'd arranged for him to do so but he didn't turn up, and I was occupied with Ignazi. I'd been away a lot and my affairs had been neglected. You can check, if you like. We were moving about the estate the whole day. Ignazi will give you the itinerary and you can check with the people we saw. I had no time that day to see anybody else.'

16

They were unable to check the Vicomte's movements with Ignazi because when they rang back to the château he'd just left to go to L'Aride at the other side of the island on business connected with the sulphur, while Tissandi was away making the rounds of the electrical appliance companies in the South of France that sold the Rapido Miniature .

'Baron Ignazi will be back late,' the clerk said. 'The sulphur always takes time. We store it, of course. The government arranged a lease for all we produce. It's top quality and they pay us a subsidy to stockpile it. Some arrangement against a possible emergency.'

Since there was little they could do, they decided to make a lazy day of it. De Troq' arranged to go swimming with Nelly who, despite her boy friend on the mainland, was more than willing to show him the best beach, and Pel took a leisurely lunch with Madame on the Duponts' verandah.

'I think Nelly's fallen for De Troq',' Madame pointed out.

'She'll get over it,' Pel said. 'Especially when De Troq' disappears, as he's bound to when this is all cleared up. She'll go back to work for the Vicomte.'

'She's not keen,' Madame said.

'Oh?' Pel looked up, suspecting something interesting. 'Why not?'

It turned out to be no more than a minor scandal – so minor, in fact, it was really only a talking point.

'Nelly says he chases the girls on his staff. He tried to chase her but she told him her boy friend was big and useful with his fists – he isn't really, but it didn't matter, it sounded good – so he's left her alone since. All the same, she fancies a change. Nevertheless – ' Madame smiled ' – I gather there's more than one child on the estate which doesn't know who its father is.'

It was very much as Pel had thought.

'Nelly knows everything that happens on the island,' Madame went on cheerfully. 'She's lived here all her life. She says there were a lot of tongues wagging about that new harbour that's been built. Everybody thought a few bribes were handed over.'

'They did?'

'She says this man at the other side of the island – a man called Rambert – a Marseilles financier, she said – was involved.'

'How did *she* find that out? It's not the sort of thing that people talk about.'

'Try to stop women gossiping. They had big parties over there and sometimes hired girls from the Vieux Port to help serve the meals. There's no one to call on at that side of the island, of course, because it's a new development and there's no village handy, so they had to get the help from this side and take them over by car.'

'Rambert.' Pel looked intrigued. 'Rambert,' he said again. 'Do you think *he's* involved?'

'He's a financier,' Pel said. 'Financiers are *always* involved. I think I'd better go and turn a few stones over and see what crawls out.'

Leaving Madame and Nelly preparing to take a picnic on the beach near Le Havre du Sud, Pel and De Troq' climbed into the car and crossed the island by the twisting roads through the olive groves. Muriel came upon them suddenly, something quite different from the Vieux Port, Le Havre du Sud or Biz. They were old, shabby island towns with a few new houses. This was a totally modern suburb.

Street lights had been erected and the streets had obviously been laid out in a large complex long before the houses had been built, because it had clearly been planned and had not grown up haphazardly like the other towns on St. Yves. Trees had been planted and were flourishing, and gardens, obviously well hosed, had been grown. It looked like a better-class suburb from somewhere on the south coast and was quite alien to the rest of the island, as if someone wanting to get away from everyday life on the mainland had started a new life on the island and made it exactly the same as the one he'd left.

Large white houses with verandahs, sunblinds and umbrellas sloped down to the beach and nearby were a few expensive boutiques of the sort that none of the islanders could ever afford to patronise. Yachts lay at anchor in the little bay and men and women in expensive clothes moved about the harbour.

Rambert's was the biggest house of the lot. There were three gardeners working on the terraces, and the door was opened by a butler in black trousers and a yellow-and-black-striped waistcoat.

'Monsieur Rambert's busy at the moment,' he said. 'He can't be disturbed.'

'I think he can,' Pel said briskly, showing his identity card. 'We're police.'

The butler didn't even blink. 'I'll ask him,' he said.

'Don't ask him,' Pel advised, his eye as sharp as a wall topped with broken glass. 'Tell him.'

The butler left them in the hall and disappeared silently. Shortly afterwards he returned. 'This way,' he said.

He led them through corridors as long as the Champs Elysées. Rambert, a fat man wearing dark glasses, was sitting at a vast desk smoking a cigar like a telegraph pole and holding a telephone to his ear. 'Buy!' he was saying. 'And don't waste time!'

Behind him, lounging on a chaise longue with a small dog on her lap, was a statuesque blonde, who gave them a smile like a toothpaste advert.

Rambert slammed down the telephone and rose, but he didn't offer his hand. 'Police, I was told,' he said.

'That's right.'

'What do you want? I'm busy at the moment.' He gestured at the woman. 'This is my – er – my wife. You'll know me, of course. Everybody knows me. Who're you? A sergeant from the Marseilles lot?'

'I'm Chief Inspector Pel,' Pel said coldly. 'And this is my associate, Baron de Troquereau.'

De Troq' did his thing, clicking his heels and giving a little bow. Rambert was obviously impressed, because he promptly offered cigars and drinks.

'What can I do for you?' he said.

'Smuggling,' Pel said.

Rambert flushed and Pel suddenly wondered if by accident he'd stumbled on something, because that was the way it sometimes went. Some dumb cop stopping a car because it had a faulty light could find the driver was some type wanted for mass-murder. And because the guy was trying to keep a low profile and look normal and innocent, he was wearing his seat belt as he should and couldn't make a quick getaway, so that the cop found he'd got a medal for the capture of Public Enemy No. 1.

But Rambert recovered quickly. 'What would I know about that?' he said. 'It's not something I go in for. I make my money in easier ways.'

'Not you, Monsieur,' Pel said blandly. 'Islanders. I understand various commodities have been known to pass through this island from Italy, via Corsica, to the mainland. We've been investigating the beaches. Your house has a magnificent view – '

'Best on the island. Chose it myself.'

'I'm wondering if you ever saw anything unusual.'

'Only that idiot, Flourmel, falling in the sea off his boat the other night when he was drunk. But I suppose it's not all that unusual. He does it about once a fortnight. It's a good job he can swim and that it sobers him up immediately.'

'No strangers about?'

'None I've ever seen.'

'No strange motor cars?'

'Most people move about by boat. It's easier than going by road. We've all got boats here, of course, or we wouldn't *be* here. That's what this place's all about. There are only about two decent cars on the island. Mine and the Vicomte de la Rochemare's.'

'You know the Vicomte?'

'Of course.' Rambert sounded indignant that Pel should even ask. 'I expect you'll meet him eventually in the course of your enquiries.'

'I've already met him,' Pel said smugly. 'In fact, you could say I've been personally appointed by him to sort out the death of the taxi-driver, Caceolari. He's put a house at my disposal.' It wasn't all quite true but it clearly impressed Rambert. 'Did *you* know Caceolari?'

'I've heard of him. His taxi never worked, I heard.'

'That seems to be him. Did he ever come to see you?'

'About what?'

'That's what I want to know. He was in trouble and he went to see someone.'

'He wouldn't come to me.'

'He might. You're a man of affairs who could give good advice.'

Rambert was flattered. 'Well, that's true. But he never did.'

Pel changed the subject. 'This is a splendid area,' he said.

Rambert beamed. 'My own idea. My own plan. I financed it.'

'All part of the development of the island, I suppose? There's a splendid harbour at the Vieux Port.'

'I fixed that, too. It was a miserable place to come into before. People won't come to that sort of place. They want a bit of glamour.'

'I gather the islanders don't like it very much.'

'Well, *they* wouldn't know their arse from their elbow when it comes to comfort, would they? Have you ever seen inside their houses? Nothing like this.'

'Perhaps they don't have as much money as you, Monsieur.'

Rambert smiled. 'Well, that's true, I suppose. But the place needed jerking into the present century. They still behave as if it were 1870 and we'd just been beaten by the Prussians. I've wakened it up, I can tell you. This place shows what can be done. Eventually, we'll start building round the Vieux Port. And then at Le Havre du Sud and Biz. There's a fortune to be made here.'

'Do the islanders want fortunes?'

'In the end they do, I've found. I've developed plenty of places. In the Balearics. On Corsica and Elba. Development brings trade and trade brings money. And give them a taste of money and they realise what they've been missing and start joining in.'

'It must have cost something.'

Rambert grinned. 'I've got something.'

'But surely you couldn't do it all on your own?'

Rambert's grin came again. 'Not likely. I don't put all my eggs in one basket and, until the islanders get the hang of it, I spread it around. I let a few others help to hold the eggs until I have the thing going. There are plenty who're willing to put up money.'

'From the mainland, I suppose? Marseilles and Nice?'

Rambert was suddenly wary. 'Some, Not all.'

'And, of course, you'd need the permission of the Ministry of Beaux Arts.'

Rambert gestured airily. 'We can get that sort of thing without difficulty.'

'Do they approve?'

'They seem to.'

Pel paused. He didn't like Rambert. He was being thoroughly impartial, of course. He normally always just settled for disliking everybody, but Rambert had the charm of Attila the Hun, so that Pel half-hoped he *was* involved in what they were investigating so that he could enjoy sending him to jail.

To make it worse, having refused Rambert's offer of a cigar, he'd just discovered that his cigarette, the last of his daytime allowance, had a split in it and, to avoid fuss, he was trying to smoke it with one finger over the tear. The effort was making his eyes stick out and his temper was shortening in proportion.

He decided to try a sneak attack while Rambert wasn't ready. 'Do you know a man called Hardy?' he asked.

It obviously succeeded. Rambert, who had been idly toying with a glass, looked up, as startled as a choirboy who suddenly discovers he's singing bass. He recovered quickly.

'Who's he?' he said. 'That politician who's involved in that enquiry?'

'That's right.'

'Why are you asking me about him?'

'I understand he had a house here.'

'Yes, he did. I sold it to him. He got rid of it about two years later.'

'Ever meet him socially?'

'Once.'

'How did that happen?'

'We gave a big party. We invited him.'

'Was he a friend of yours then?'

'No, but you know how it is.'

'No, I don't. Inform me.'

'Well, in my profession, you keep your ear close to the ground. It pays to know the right people and politicians are the right people. It pays to be seen with people like that. So we included him.'

'Just once?'

'Just once. I never saw him again, as far as I know. He didn't return the invitation. Then I went to America on business. Soon afterwards he sold the house.'

'What about a man called Tagliatti? Maurice Tagliatti?'

Rambert had become very still. 'Isn't that the gangster chap?' he asked.

'Yes.'

'What are you suggesting?'

Pel had a feeling that he'd got another bite. 'Nothing, Monsieur,' he said. 'I thought perhaps one of your staff might have been involved and you might have heard his name mentioned.'

'My staff are absolutely loyal to me.'

'Of course. *Did* you know Tagliatti?'

Rambert hesitated. 'Everybody in Marseilles knew about Tagliatti.'

'That wasn't what I asked. I asked did you *know* him?'

Rambert suddenly looked shifty. 'Well, as a matter of fact, yes, though I don't go around boasting about it. We grew up together and went to the same school. I played in goal and he was right-wing. He's left the country.'

'So I understand.'

'Tax problems. Everybody has those. He's in Switzerland. He always goes to Switzerland for that. He's a fugitive from the Inland Revenue but that doesn't count as a crime, does it?'

Though Rambert laughed at his joke, Pel didn't.

'Was he involved with the casinos in Nice?' he asked. 'There's been trouble over them.'

'He had interests in one of them.'

'How about you?'

'How about me what?'

'Did *you* have interests in them?'

Rambert shifted in his seat. 'I'd like to see them operating again, of course. But I'm not involved. Except with a little money, but there's nothing wrong with that, is there?'

Pel managed a smile. It was as dry as old chicken bones. He rose. 'Well, I imagine this isn't the place where we'll find our smugglers, Monsieur.'

'I shouldn't think so. There are plenty of crooks, of course.' Rambert laughed. 'But not that kind.'

'Have you ever been threatened, Monsieur?'

Rambert's face fell. 'What with?'

'Houses have been set alight. Holiday homes. A lot, as a matter of fact. By someone on the island who doesn't approve of people coming here from the mainland and taking the place over. What you might call a sort of mini-nationalism.'

'They'd better not try it here,' Rambert growled. 'I have dogs around the garden after dark. If anybody comes they bark as if Cossacks were sacking the place. Besides, I thought the objection was to the people who've taken over houses that were already here and converted them to holiday homes. I haven't converted anything. I built. From the ground up. For a different class of people. The islanders can't afford my homes. St. Yves is a good place to live.'

'That's probably what the islanders feel, Monsieur.' Pel smiled and rose. 'I should take great care.'

They left Rambert looking uneasy. As they stepped on to the porch, the blank-faced butler was polishing the handle of the door. There was something ostentatious about the way he was doing it, as if he were there deliberately. Sure enough he was.

'Have a word with Luz Robles,' he murmured as he closed the door. 'She knows.'

'Knows what?'

'What the old bastard's been up to.'

He'd obviously been eavesdropping on the questioning and Pel smiled as he climbed into the car. So much for the loyalty of Rambert's staff.

17

When Ignazi returned, it wasn't hard to check that what the Vicomte had said was true. Ignazi still had the itinerary that he'd prepared. It included the vineyard, the olive groves, the farms, the freezer plant, the sulphur, the hotel, everything the Vicomte owned on the island.

'He makes a point of keeping an eye on them all,' Ignazi said 'Personally.'

Judging by the times, it seemed unlikely that the Vicomte *had* had time to see Caceolari and when De Troq' did a little checking everything that the Vicomte had said seemed to be true.

So if it weren't the Vicomte Caceolari had seen, who had it been? They went back to Tissandi. If Caceolari hadn't seen the Vicomte, could Tissandi have seen him?

'Sure,' Tissandi said. 'I saw him.'

They were standing in the warehouse behind the château, surrounded by chattering girls and acres of paper and corrugated card, watching the packing of the japanned boxes and Rapido Minis. Tissandi wore the same casual clothes as everybody else but there was nothing rough and ready about them and he made Pel feel like the man who came to empty the dustbins.

'So he did come?' Pel said.

'Oh, yes,' Tissandi agreed cheerfully. 'He came. He seemed anxious to talk to me.'

'What did he say?'

'Nothing.' Tissandi looked puzzled.

'Was he worried?'

Tissandi considered for a moment before replying. 'Yes,' he said. 'I would say he *was* worried and I tried to get out of him what he was worried about. But he was vague. Very vague. I couldn't make out what it was all about.'

'Did you do anything about it?'

'What could I have done?'

'You could have reported it to the police.'

'To Beauregard?' Tissandi smiled.

Pel saw the point. 'There were always the police on the mainland,' he said.

'I didn't really think it was that important. I didn't even understand what he was afraid of.'

'But if he was afraid, he would surely have reason to be.'

'I suppose that's true.'

'But you did nothing?'

Tissandi shrugged. 'I wasn't even sure it was a matter for the police,' he said. 'He was so vague, it might even have been a family matter. Something between him and his wife. Something of that sort. It was as if he wanted to tell me something but hadn't the courage and could only hint. I thought about it then let it go. And arranged that he should see the Vicomte when he returned. He was to have seen him on the 23rd. The Vicomte's a busy man, of course, and these things have to be fitted in. But before then, of course, Caceolari was dead.'

Indeed he was. And someone knew why.

But the interview with Rambert had opened up a whole new field of interest, and Pel was certain he was involved somewhere in what was going on. Nobody as sharp and shrewd – and crafty – as he was could fail to be.

It seemed to be time to see Madame Robles again. He'd always intended to and at the second time of asking sometimes people remembered.

Luz Robles greeted Pel more warmly than the first time. Without asking, she pulled out chairs and produced a bottle.

Pel gestured at De Troq'. 'This is Baron de Troquereau.'

De Troq' smiled his aloof smile, clicked his heels, gave a little bow, grabbed Madame Robles' hand and kissed it. She was clearly very impressed and kept her eyes on him all the time they were speaking.

'My Cousin Eugenia married a baron,' she said. 'An Italian baron. But he was a bit shifty. He had no money and when he'd spent all hers he left her. I could have told her the minute I met him.' She looked at Pel. 'But you didn't come here to talk about my Cousin Eugenia. What do you want?'

'Do you know Rambert?' Pel asked. 'The financier type at the other side of the island.'

She was immediately wary. 'Why should I know Rambert?' she asked.

'He has money. He has style.' Pel paused. 'You have style.'

She seemed flattered and he went on. 'I'd have thought that people of style on an island like this where there isn't a *lot* of style would naturally gravitate together.'

Madame Robles smiled. 'You'd be surprised how much style there is during the summer. It comes in on the yachts.'

'It doesn't seem to have spread to the islanders.'

'Well, it wouldn't, would it? You know how it is. The islanders are suspicious of money. They think they're wealthy if they can afford a new car or a new suit, if they have three cows instead of two. They don't know what wealth is. Wealth is what *they* keep in a sock under the bed and they turn up for weddings in vans and trucks because a car would be an extravagance when they've already got something on wheels. They *don't* have style. The people who come in yachts know how to behave.'

'Do they come *here*? To this bar?'

'Sometimes. More often than not they go to the hotel.'

'Do you go there?'

'Sometimes.'

'When Rambert's there?'

'I have done.'

'So you do know him?'

She flushed. 'Yes, I know him.'

'It might have saved time,' Pel said dryly, 'if you'd said that when I first asked.'

She recovered quickly. 'You people have to work for your living,' she said sharply. 'You can't expect to have things handed to you on a plate.'

'There is such a thing,' Pel retorted coldly, 'as refusing to help the police. Now, Madame, shall we start again? Do you know Rambert?'

'Yes.'

'Well?'

'Yes.'

'Well enough to visit his house?'

'I have done.'

'Have you ever been threatened with having *your* house burned down?'

'I live here. All the time. I don't just come occasionally.'

'What about Rambert? He doesn't live here all the time.'

'There's a permanent staff there. With guard dogs. They wouldn't burn that down, would they?'

'Does Rambert ever come here?'

'Of course not.'

'I thought he might. In fact, I've been informed he might.'

He hadn't, but it was worth trying and she immediately looked uneasy. 'Well, he has once or twice.'

'Why?'

'Why does anyone come to a bar?'

'I don't think Rambert's the type to drink in a bar like this.'

'What's wrong with it?'

'It's not big enough and glossy enough for Rambert. Did he come to see you, Madame?'

She didn't answer and Pel pressed the question. In the end she nodded.

'How well do you know him?'

'How well do you think?'

'I can guess.'

She gestured irritably. 'That blonde he's got there,' she said. 'She's not his wife, of course. His wife's in Marseilles. They can't stand each other. He took up with the blonde and now he's sick of her, too. She's got the brains of that poodle she nurses all day. Rambert's got drive. He needs intelligence.'

'And something else?'

'And something else,' she admitted defiantly.

'Ever meet a man called Hardy?'

'Who's he?'

'He's a politician. You may have read of him.'

She frowned. 'Once Rambert brought someone here who might have been him. They didn't introduce him to me. But I heard them talking. He sounded as if he might have been a politician. Things he said. References to the House of Representatives. That sort of thing.'

138

'You said, "they" didn't introduce him. Who are "they"?'

'Well, Rambert and this other man.'

'Which other man?'

'The one that came with him.'

'Would it have been Maurice Tagliatti?'

She hesitated for a long time before answering. 'Yes,' she admitted.

'Do you know him?'

'A little. He's been here, too. But not lately. He's gone to Switzerland.'

'So I heard. Why did he come here?'

'I don't know. Rambert always brought him.'

It was Pel's turn to be silent for a while. So both Tagliatti and Hardy had interests on the island. And they seemed to be the same interests as those of Rambert, who was obviously not anxious to be associated with them. Which was doubtless why they used Luz Robles' bar in the hills instead of the bar of the hotel in the Vieux Port where they might have expected better service and greater comfort.

'Did Tagliatti put up any of the money for the estate at Muriel?' It was more than likely because it was well known that, having made his pile from shady deals, Tagliatti was now trying to appear respectable.

Madame Robles nodded. 'He has a house there.'

'Does he indeed? What about the harbour at the Vieux Port? Does he have any interests there?'

'He part-owns the hotel.'

Pel shifted his position. Things were growing interesting. There was nothing they could accuse anybody of yet but it was safe to assume if Tagliatti was in on any business deals they were shady ones, which seemed to suggest that Rambert's – and Hardy's – could be shady, too. Perhaps they were connected with a few other names the police were interested in. And were Tagliatti and his boys up to something on the island, and had Caceolari discovered what it was and had he been threatening blackmail?

'Caceolari,' Pel said.

Madame Robles looked sullen. 'I've already talked about him.'

'Let's talk about him again. When he came to see you the

139

night before he died, you told me he mentioned that shooting on the mainland.'

'Yes, he did.'

'Did he seem to know something about it?'

She gave him a quick look. 'I think he did. I never thought about it until now. I just thought he was nervous that perhaps the people who'd done it had hidden on the island or something.'

'They might have done,' Pel said quietly.

She gave him a sharp look. 'Thanks for the warning. I'll make sure I lock my doors at night. Where are they?'

Pel ignored the question. 'Why do you think he was nervous?'

'Just the way he went on about it. I got the impression he'd seen something.'

'Did he say what?'

'No.'

Pel knew she was lying. He'd had enough experience of lying to recognise it at once.

'I think you can do better than that,' he said.

'What do you mean?'

'I think he *did* tell you.'

'No. No, he didn't.'

'Would you be prepared to come down to the police station and swear to that? Perhaps even go to Nice and swear to it there?'

She stared at Pel. 'I think he saw guns,' she said.

'Where?'

'In a boat that came into the harbour. The night those men were shot down in Nice. He saw *one*, anyway. He said it was covered by a tarpaulin but that the tarpaulin snagged on something and pulled away.'

Pel glanced at De Troq'. 'It must have been a big gun to have to carry it under a tarpaulin,' he said.

'He said it was a sub-machine gun. A tommy gun.'

'Only the army, the police and certain security organisations are allowed sub-machine guns,' Pel said slowly. 'Did he say who was in the boat?'

'He said there were three.'

'But he didn't recognise them?'

'He didn't say so.'

140

'Do you know a man called Riccio? He keeps a restaurant in the Vieux Port.'

'I've heard of it. I gather it's not very good.'

Pel was inclined to agree and she went on, almost as if suddenly she were pleased to get things off her chest. 'When I eat out I use Luigi's or the hotel,' she said. 'They're much better. These little places are a bit scruffy.' Remembering the charcoal and the fish, Pel was inclined to agree with that too. 'But I didn't know him,' she said. 'I wouldn't know him from Adam.'

'Maquin?'

'Who's he?'

'Friend of Riccio's.'

'No.'

'And the third man? Who was he?'

'Caceolari didn't say.'

Pel paused. 'This boat Caceolari saw. What happened to it? Did he say anything about that?'

'He said it came into the harbour then went away again towards the north. I said where could it go to the north? There's only Biz. He said it probably went back to Nice.'

Pel rose. As he reached the door, she smiled nervously, as if relieved that the questioning was over. 'When I go to Nice,' she said, 'I'll be able to dine out on this for weeks.'

Pel turned quickly. 'I think you'd be better advised to keep it to yourself,' he said. 'It might be safer.'

She looked startled. 'You think someone will shoot *me* or something.'

Pel sniffed. Marseilles was full of Corsicans and the Union de Corse and the Corsican Mafia was reputed – though nobody was ever certain – to have its headquarters and its most powerful influence there.

'If it was the Marseilles lot Caceolari saw,' he said quietly, 'they well might.'

18

Things suddenly began to look different.

'A good catch,' Pel murmured thoughtfully. 'Caceolari told his wife it was heavy and Riccio himself said they'd done well, yet, though he had a freezer, all he had when we arrived a few days later was swordfish. Frozen swordfish. We took our very first meal in that restaurant and that was all he could offer us.'

'Swordfish was all he could *ever* offer us,' Madame commented.

'He obviously wasn't such a good fisherman as he claimed,' De Troq' smiled.

'Or perhaps he didn't use his boat much for fishing.' Pel leaned forward. 'When we asked why he had nothing but swordfish he said it was because all the fresh fish had been eaten. But Madame Caceolari said the islanders didn't eat in his restaurant because it was too expensive and we were the first tourists to go there. He said so. He hadn't been open until then. And I've never seen many since.' Pel looked at his wife. 'So why didn't he have mullet, or tunny or pilchards? What happened to this famous catch he'd made? Could it be that he hadn't been fishing at all?'

Madame was finally beginning to get the drift of the way they were thinking. 'This is much more exciting than watching elderly ladies having their hair done,' she admitted. 'Elderly ladies with wet hair aren't the prettiest sight, anyway.'

They sat outside the bar near Riccio's, their eyes on Riccio's door. Three tourists had turned up from Biz on motor scooters and they could see Riccio moving about inside preparing food – without doubt, swordfish.

Pel was quiet, deep in thought. Why had Riccio been so friendly with Jean-Bernard Fleurie and his friends from

142

Tagliatti's gang? Was it simply that he'd *always* been friendly with young Fleurie? After all, he might *not* have known his friends were gangsters. Gangsters didn't go around with little buttons in their lapels indicating their profession. On the other hand, island gossip being what it was, there was a good chance that he *did* know what Fleurie was involved in and, if so, that he also knew what his companions did for a living.

There was certainly *something* going on from the island and it began to seem that Jean-Bernard had brought Tagliatti into it, with the encouragement of whoever it was who was behind it, and that Caceolari had stumbled on it.

'It's fairly clear,' he said, 'that what Caceolari saw that night he'd been with Magimel was Riccio's boat coming into the harbour and that what Riccio was carrying ashore was not fish, as he told us, and not a body – but guns. From that we assume with some safety that, since it was the night those six were shot in the Bar-Tabac de la Porte in Nice, that that's where the guns came from.'

'Think it was a gang wipe-out, Patron?' De Troq' asked. 'Was Tagliatti muscling in on somebody else's territory?'

'If that was it,' Pel asked, 'why didn't Tagliatti's mob respond? Even in Switzerland he wouldn't let his men be bumped off without hitting back twice as hard.' He was on the point of lighting another cigarette when he suddenly shook out the match and sat staring in front of him at the boats bobbing in the harbour.

'Are you all right?' Madame asked.

'Of course!' Pel came to life abruptly. 'It wasn't the opposition who wiped out those six. *It was Tagliatti himself!* It must have been! So why? There must have been a good reason.'

'The best one I can think of, Patron,' De Troq' said, 'is that they'd done something he didn't like. These gangs demand tight discipline.'

'And that's why they used guns. Their usual method of getting rid of people is to bake them in a concrete cake and drop them in the harbour or place them under a new motorway.' As Madame winced, Pel patted her hand. 'But this time it was guns. And with a lot of publicity. They must have been trying to put something across him and he wanted to make sure everybody else who worked for him would get the message and not try the same trick. So he had it done this way to make it loud and clear.'

De Troq' frowned. 'It's something we'll never prove, Patron,' he said. 'There'll be half a dozen people between Tagliatti and whoever did it.'

'But not a lot between *us* and the types who did it, because we already know Riccio was involved. Was he one of Tagliatti's informers? Did he pass on some information he'd picked up to Tagliatti's hit men? Did he find out that Jean-Bernard and his friends were up to something Tagliatti wouldn't have approved of? He must have been part of the business because you've only to look at him to see he's obviously not expecting any reaction from anybody, as he would be if he'd been involved with some other outfit and set up the shootings for *them*. *He* must be working for Tagliatti, too.'

He paused, deep in thought. 'Those six were merely errand boys,' he went on after a while. 'They were probably responsible for seeing whatever it was that was being moved came safely into the country. Perhaps they'd been helping themselves and Riccio found out. Jean-Bernard boasted to his mother that he'd just done well out of some deal. Perhaps he boasted of it to Riccio. Perhaps Riccio's one of Tagliatti's shadows. The types he pays to keep an eye on his boys. But if he was, Jean-Bernard didn't know. Otherwise they'd hardly boast about putting something across Tagliatti which, it seems, is what they *were* doing when Jean-Bernard's mother saw them from her window. So it got back to Tagliatti and – paf! – ' Pel slapped his knee with the flat of his hand ' – that was that! They didn't know it but they'd just signed their own death warrants.'

He paused and sipped his pernod. 'Perhaps Riccio was used to get the weapons away afterwards. None were ever found, and Riccio arrived back here with the guns some time after 2.30 a.m. It would fit. He went out during the afternoon. He said so. He could have been waiting off Nice for one of Tagliatti's launches – I'm sure he's got some – to bring them out to him, then he left Nice immediately and headed back to sea. Perhaps Tagliatti had arranged beforehand for him to hide them. After all, no weapons, no charges. It's an old dodge. Get rid of the weapons and you're safe.'

'Perhaps it was bigger than that,' Madame suggested. She

had been listening quietly, ignored by the other two in the excitement of what they'd learned, and they turned quickly to look at her.

'Bigger than that?' Pel said.

'Much bigger.'

'How much bigger?'

'Bigger by a murder. Six murders?'

De Troq's eyebrows shot up. 'You think Riccio did it?'

Pel studied his wife for a moment then he turned to De Troq'. 'Why not?' he asked.

'On Tagliatti's orders?'

'Why not?' Pel said again. 'Perhaps he went to Nice especially. It wouldn't be difficult. Six hours there and six hours back. It takes the ferry five and the ferry's faster than anything else in the harbour.'

'Wouldn't the harbourmaster in Nice report his boat? They do everywhere else.'

'Perhaps they didn't go into Nice. Perhaps they anchored well offshore and were picked up by a fast Tagliatti launch. Once on dry land, they could have been driven into the city, done the job, been driven back and been taken out to their boat, and set off home. They'd be out of the city before the road blocks were set up and at sea before anybody noticed. It would take them at least until 2.30 a.m. to get back. It has all the stamp of Tagliatti's way of working and would account for all those splendid alibis the police found. Tagliatti's boys had good alibis for the simple reason that they weren't there. They simply provided the means for Riccio to get clear. The rest Riccio attended to himself.'

It began to seem a distinct possibility.

'After all,' Pel said, 'Caceolari saw three men in a boat – Riccio, Maquin and one other. We know that. There were three men in that bar shooting. Was it Riccio and Maquin and this other man? Perhaps Riccio rubbed them out for Tagliatti and, because Caceolari, who'd been drinking with the Robles woman at Mortcerf and with Magimel, the farmer, was late getting home, he saw them arrive and saw the guns. When he read of the murders next day he put two and two together and made a guess. And *they* guessed he'd guessed. Perhaps even they found out that he saw them.'

'How, Patron? Who passed on the information that he'd

seen them? Caceolari was wary. He told Luz Robles he saw guns but he mentioned no names. To his wife he only said he saw Riccio and mentioned no guns. So how did Riccio learn he'd seen them with the guns? *Somebody* knew. And we still have to find out who.'

Nevertheless Pel patted his wife's hand. 'I think we've suddenly begun to make progress.'

19

The following evening the police in Marseilles picked up a
seventeen-year-old boy who had died of an overdose of heroin.

He had been found in a basement flat, half-starved. He
had left home some time before and instead of spending his
money on food he'd been spending it on drugs and had been
living in the basement room for some time. Alongside him
was a syringe and the small paper packet which had contained
his fix.

It was enough to alert the police and later that night, Jean-
Bernard Fleurie's girl, Madeleine Rou, who worked at the
Kit Kat Klub, a sleazy joint near the harbour, not as the
boss's secretary as Madame Fleurie thought, but as one of
the strippers, was spotted handing over a small parcel to one
of the other girls. Though the owner hadn't known it, the
club was full of cops and they had pounced at once.

Madeleine Rou and the other girl were charged with being
in possession of drugs. They strenuously denied it and the
girl who had accepted the drugs had hurriedly shoved the
packet behind a group of wine bottles behind the bar. But
when tested, they were both found to have traces of the drug
on their hands.

'It's something you can't get off,' Inspector Maillet pointed
out cheerfully. 'It's always a great help.'

Both girls were hostile and unhelpful at first but as Maillet
began to lean on them and talk of long sentences, they broke
down. The drugs had come from Jean-Bernard.

That was all Madeleine Rou knew. The other girl was the
go-between for a man who peddled drugs on the streets and,
when he was brought in, too, he didn't know anything either.
He just took the drug, broke it down into sizeable doses and
sold it where it was needed.

It was the same old story. Everything was sewn up tighter

than the old Resistance réseaux of wartime France. No one knew who was involved beyond the next one in the line. That way, the people at the top who organised things never got raked in or had to answer charges.

All Madeleine Rou knew about the drugs was that Jean-Bernard Fleurie, La Petite Fleur, had produced them, told her to hide them and pass them on later when and where he told her to. Since he was no longer there to help and since she needed money she had done the next best thing. Having asked around, she had found that one of her co-strippers at the Kit Kat Klub knew people who were involved with drugs so she'd arranged to hand it over at what was, it turned out, a staggeringly low price. When she learned how much the drugs were worth, Madeleine Rou turned on her co-stripper and might have attacked her but for the presence of the police. As it was, she treated her to the length of her tongue and a promise to get her later for swindling her. The other girl insisted that she, too, hadn't known the value and had offered only what she'd been told. At which point, Madeleine Rou turned on the man who was to have taken possession from the other girl, and this time it ended up in a free-for-all that had required three policemen to sort out.

The thing that intrigued the police, however, was the shape of the bags that Madeleine Rou had tried to hand over. Normally heroin came in plastic bags about twenty centimetres long and ten centimetres wide, which was a useful size for stuffing into the nooks and crannies of motor cars, caravans and other vehicles. These bags were only fifteen centimetres long and about four centimetres across. Obviously they didn't hold as much as the normal ones but nobody was kidding that there weren't more

When the police launch from Nice arrived in the harbour of the Vieux Port, Pel was waiting for it with the Duponts' car and he went on board at once to see Inspector Maillet who had asked for a conference.

'It came from here,' Maillet said at once. 'I'm sure of that.'

'Proof?' Pel asked.

'None. It's just a guess.'

'Well, never mind,' Pel said. 'There are a few people we'll

be wanting to pick up here before long. They'll probably talk. Did you bring search warrants?'

'We did. They took some getting because officially the judiciary on the mainland has no authority here but we managed to get the rules waived. Quietly. It'll be good enough to make a search, though there'll be a hell of a row if we find nothing.'

Pel nodded. 'Then we'd better find *something*,' he said.

They drove across the island to Muriel, De Troq' handling the big car as if it were his roadster. His style shook Maillet and even Pel, who was used to it, looked vaguely uneasy.

De Troq' had already discovered which was Tagliatti's house but when they arrived it was locked up, the doors and windows barred. An old man was working in the garden.

'He isn't here,' he said.

'We know that,' Maillet said. He produced the search warrant and demanded that the door be opened. 'Have you got a key?'

'Well, yes, I have,' the old man said. 'But I was told to let nobody in.'

Maillet flashed his identity card. 'We're the police and we have good reason for wanting to see inside. Open up.'

The house was built on the same lines as Rambert's, with rooms big enough to play polo in without damaging the fittings. The furnishings were luxurious and the paintings were modern and looked just as expensive. They went through the place from top to bottom, replacing everything carefully. There were clothes in the wardrobes and more in the drawers, one room full of women's garments.

'Wonder who the lucky lady is,' Maillet said.

They found wines of a sort that none of them had ever dared consider drinking – it would have been sacrilege even to open the bottle – occasional bundles of high-denomination notes in the drawers, as if they'd been thrown in and forgotten – and in the garage a large Citroën like the Vicomte's, polished until it shone, but cold and obviously not used for some time.

'Makes you wonder how they get away with it, doesn't it,' Maillet observed.

There was nothing by which they could connect Maurice Tagliatti to the drugs in Nice, however. They weren't really surprised. They knew Tagliatti to be far too clever to leave things about.

'He probably has his own private detective to go round after him,' Maillet said ruefully. 'Some bent cop who's employed to make sure there are no give-aways left lying about.'

It was disappointing but only what they'd expected, and they returned to Maillet's boat in silence.

'There's one other angle,' Pel said. 'Riccio. He's involved. What's his background?'

Maillet's assistant had looked him up. He opened a file. 'Salvatore Riccio,' he said. 'Known as Turidu Riccio. Background: Paras. He was used in North Africa while he was still very young on secret missions that seem usually to have resulted in some awkward Algerian being removed from the scene.'

'A hit man?' Pel glanced quickly at De Troq'. 'That makes sense.'

'We think now – now that we've turned this up – that he's been used before, in gang murders in Marseilles and Paris. We've had Tagliatti's deputy in and chewed him up, of course, but we got nowhere. Tagliatti, of course, is in Switzerland.'

'Tagliatti,' Pel said, remembering his own encounter with the gangster, 'would ride something like this without turning a hair. He has nothing to fear, I dare bet. What about Maquin?'

Maillet picked up another file. 'Also Paras. Not with Riccio. But I bet Riccio would recognise another Para straight away and recruit him. He's a dead shot with a rifle. He's known to have helped with game shoots on the mainland.'

'He's known to have helped with them here too,' Pel said.

Maillet looked puzzled. 'But they removed Caceolari with a knife,' he pointed out.

Pel shrugged. 'A knife's quieter.'

'And how did they find out he'd seen them?'

'We still have to sort that one out.'

'Will you want us to help?'

'No.' Pel shook his head. 'We'll handle it ourselves.'

'Got enough men?'

Pel smiled. 'We'll make it enough,' he said. 'We'll tackle it tomorrow evening and we'd like the helicopter here the day after to take away the catch.'

*

150

That night, however, there were complications. There was another burning.

This time it was a small cottage at Biz belonging to a retired couple from Nice called Vésin. They had put their savings into it and lived in a flat for the rest of the year so they could enjoy the solitude of the island during the summer when the south coast of France grew too busy with tourists. Since Beauregard seemed unwilling to do much, Pel decided to take a look.

The cottage's white walls were blackened by smoke and the roof had fallen into a mass of burnt timbers and cracked tiles, on which Lesage and his men were pumping water from the swimming pool. A large fig tree that overhung it was scarred by the flames and one or two local people were staring at it, picking up odds and ends. One man was about to make off with a rake when Pel stopped him.

'Where are you going with that?'

'Well, *they* won't want it, will they? Not now.'

'Have you asked them?'

'No.'

'Then put it back.'

The man stared Pel full in the face. 'And who might you be?'

De Troq' grinned. 'For your information, this is Chief Inspector Pel, Brigade Criminelle, Police Judiciaire. And he does his job rather better than Brigadier Beauregard. If I were you, I *would* put it back.'

The man dropped the rake as if it were red hot and scuttled off. Obviously one or two of the others had also been prowling round for what they could pick up and they began to shuffle off, too.

They moved towards the building. There was a little garage built on the back and as the roof of the cottage had collapsed it had brought down the roof of the garage. A man was poking about in the debris with a fork and they recognised him as Oudry, the baker from Biz, Caceolari's brother-in-law.

'Looking for something, Monsieur?' Pel asked.

'My property, that's all.' Oudry raised his pasty face to them.

'What property would that be?'

Oudry shrugged. 'Tools. Things like that. We're short of

space at home and Madame Vésin gave me permission to store them in their garage while they're away. We had a key and kept an eye on the place. They paid us for it. I was going to remove them before their first let in June.' He shrugged. 'It won't be necessary now. There won't be anything left.'

Calling on Beauregard in his office, Pel found him engaged in writing a laborious report on the new arson case. He looked bored but his boredom vanished at once as Pel informed him that he'd come across a hint of smuggling at Le Havre du Sud, and that he was to stand by in his office until he received a telephone call informing him where to meet Pel who was laying on a raid later that evening.

Beauregard looked interested. 'Where will it be, Chief?'

'I won't know until the last minute,' Pel said. 'I'll inform you by telephone.'

As they left the office, he heard the telephone click. 'He'll be spreading the word that we're coming,' Pel said. 'And everybody in Le Havre du Sud who's ever done any smuggling will be stuffing away anything illegal they possess within minutes. In the meantime, you and I will pick up Riccio and the Nice boys can tackle Maquin. I suspect Riccio'll be the awkward one. Beauregard can help us.'

'Can we trust him?'

'He won't know until it's too late and we might kill two birds with one stone. Inform the Marseilles boys that Maquin's not to be allowed near the telephone. We don't want anyone spreading the gospel and I don't want to move on Riccio until I feel we have good reason to.'

Madame Pel looked from one to the other. 'You're going to arrest someone, aren't you?'

'That depends,' Pel said, 'on whether we find anything or not.'

Pel and De Troq' took their apéritifs on the harbour and in no time were in conversation with the three young men in jeans who, by this time, had hired two-stroke motor bikes to get around. They talked together for a long time, laughing a lot to hide what was being said, then De Troq' and Pel returned to where Madame Pel had provided an excellent meal.

'This looks as if it were hard work,' De Troq' said gallantly.

'Oh, no,' she said, with equal gallantry. 'Nelly's very good and a lot of it comes out of tins. It's amazing what you can do these days. We didn't go in for anything elaborate in case you were delayed and it was spoiled.'

After the meal, they studied the photographs from the Ballistic Department that De Troq' had brought back with him, while Madame and Nelly stacked the dishes in the Duponts' dishwasher. As they finished they found Madame looking over their shoulders and obviously itching to know what it was all about. Pel explained how in firearm identification the cartridge case and the bullet itself always had clear marks on them. Several ejected cartridge cases had been picked up in the Bar-Tabac de la Porte in Marseilles and photographed under microscopes, and each one bore the imprint in considerable detail of every minute mechanical imperfection of the weapon that had fired it, from the firing pin and breech block to the ejector.

'They mean nothing, of course,' he said. 'Unless we find the gun that fired them.'

'Ordinary 9mm. bullets from a pistol were found in the bar walls,' De Troq' went on. 'It's believed they were fired with the express purpose of making the bar staff and customers keep their heads down while the type with the Sterling polished off the opposition at the counter.'

The telephone went soon after it grew dark. It was Claverie, one of the cops from Nice. 'We've got him,' he said. 'He has a 9mm. pistol which he can't account for. It's been cleaned recently, which suggests it's also been fired recently. There's also an old army revolver big enough to bring down an aircraft. First World War, I reckon.'

'Did he get to the telephone?'

'Nowhere near it, Chief. I'm speaking on it now. I think he'd like to strangle me.'

'Good. Keep your eye on him. Don't let him out of your sight.' Pel slammed the telephone down. 'Come on, De Troq'. Let's go and get Riccio before the jungle telegraph gets to work.'

Riccio had just finished cooking and a few last tourists were finishing their wine. Standing in the shadows among the boats on the slipway, Pel indicated the bar nearby.

'Go in there, De Troq',' he said. 'Use their telephone and inform Beauregard that he's needed here and tell him why.'

When De Troq' came back, Pel raised an eyebrow. 'What did he say?'

De Troq' grinned. 'He seemed startled, Patron. He said he'd be here in two or three minutes.'

'I'll bet it's nearer five,' Pel said. 'At this moment, I dare bet he's telephoning Riccio.'

As they watched from among the shadows near the boats, sure enough they heard the telephone go in Riccio's restaurant, then they saw Riccio suddenly start chivvying his customers out, yelling at them that he had to close.

'We haven't finished,' one of the men said.

'Yes, you have! I've just shut the place up!'

Pel smiled. 'Come on, De Troq',' he said.

As they stepped into the light of the restaurant doorway, Riccio saw them. For a second he stared, then leapt for the back door leading to the yard. But De Troq' was too quick. Snatching up one of the chairs he hurled it at Riccio. It caught him in the legs just as he reached the door and brought him down. As he fell, he sent one of the tables flying. A glass crashed against the wall and the tourists leapt up, the women screaming. As Riccio struggled to his feet, De Troq' wrenched his arm up behind him.

'What's going on?' one of the tourists demanded. 'What is this? A robbery?'

'Hardly,' Pel said. 'We're the police.'

Beauregard came panting up just as they found a Sterling sub-machine gun, well-greased and wrapped in rags, under a pile of sacks stuffed into a space beneath a loose floorboard in one of the outhouses at the back of the yard. His tunic was buttoned incorrectly and he was still hitching at his rusty gun in its unpolished holster on his belt.

'You took your time,' Pel snapped.

'I came as soon as I could, Chief.'

Upstairs in Riccio's bedroom, where they also found a girl of about sixteen, who turned out to be a German holiday-maker, they found 9mm. ammunition in boxes and several empty magazines for the Sterling. There was also a 9mm. pistol and a commando type dagger.

'That'll be what did for Caceolari,' De Troq' said.

'Not on your life,' Pel said. '*That'll* be in the harbour somewhere.' He turned to Beauregard. 'Right, Brigadier, you're going to have company in your cells tonight. And you'd better make sure they don't escape. Come to think of it – ' Pel looked at De Troq' ' – under the circumstances and since these types are badly wanted and we've got plenty of help, we'll have Claverie, Lebrun and Mangin sit up on guard with them.'

20

It wasn't the helicopter that came from Marseilles, but the launch. It took away Riccio and Maquin, as well as Beauregard and one of his constables. The constable had admitted that things had happened, bribes had been taken and blind eyes had been turned and, in a fury, Beauregard, anxious that the constable should share in any delights that were going, returned the compliment. It also took away the three detective sergeants from Nice, all cheerful and very pleased with themselves.

Pel watched them go. Lebrun was in no doubt that the weapons they'd found were the ones which had committed the butchery in the Bar-Tabac de la Porte. As the boat left, Pel turned to see a large Citroën which he recognised as the Vicomte de la Rochemare's standing just behind them. As he turned away, the Vicomte beckoned him. The door of the car opened and the Vicomte gestured at the half-acre of plastic tables and chairs.

'I think we need a drink, Chief Inspector,' he said.

Pel felt the occasion warranted it – even, perhaps, a cigarette, too. After all, they'd taken another step forward in the march against crime. He had spent half the night and part of the morning doing the paperwork necessary to commit Riccio, Maquin, Beauregard and his constable to the arms of the Nice police and, liking paper work no more than any other cop, had smoked enough cigarettes in the preparation of the documents to turn his lungs to cinders. He ordered a beer to wash away the ashes and they sat back, enjoying the sunshine, Pel thoroughly pleased with himself. His Honour General Baron Pel. Charles de Gaulle Pel. Foxy Pel. Lone Wolf Pel. He was all of them at once. And the triumph made him feel he'd hit back at the island for getting him there.

'I have to congratulate you, Chief Inspector,' the Vicomte

156

said. 'When I asked you to help, I didn't really expect such a quick or such a dramatic result.'

Neither had Pel but he didn't mention that.

'I knew Riccio, of course. Not personally, of course, but as a restaurateur. Whenever I had unwanted visitors in my home – politicians, tourists, the sort of people who result from chance meetings – Tissandi arranged for him to put on a dinner at his restaurant for them. Tissandi arranged for supplies to come from the château and Riccio did it quite well. It pleased them, of course, because his place has the island atmosphere that the hotel doesn't have. Perhaps more than my own place which, after all, you can see repeated ad nauseam up and down the Loire. But this – !' He shook his head in wonderment. 'And Beauregard, too! No wonder we never seemed to get anywhere with the smuggling on the island. What'll happen now?'

'I suspect,' Pel said, 'that before long you're going to have some difficulty over your laws here. As you'll doubtless remember, General de Gaulle was once all set to take over Monaco if it didn't fall into line with French thinking, and I suspect your police force, from now on, will be nominated – *and supervised* – by Nice.'

'Perhaps it's a good thing. What about you?'

'I shall now continue my holiday. In peace, I hope.'

The Vicomte laughed. 'I hope so, too,' he said. 'Perhaps you and your wife will do me the honour of dining with me one night.'

Pel thought they might. Madame would certainly be intrigued by the gold plates. It would give her something to talk about with her friends for weeks to come.

When Lebrun telephoned, the call came through to Beauregard's office, at that moment occupied by Pel and De Troq'. A search through Beauregard's desk had brought to light a lot of odd things. It seemed that the brigadier had been taking bribes for a long time – who from it wasn't clear, but they found clear proof, because Beauregard was a careful man where his finances were concerned and had set it all down. An examination of his bank account would undoubtedly show far more than a police brigadier ought to have and doubtless there were also other bank accounts that would turn up later.

157

Lebrun sounded pleased with himself. 'The Sterling and the two 9mm. Lugers matched the ejected cases found in the Bar-Tabac de la Porte and Riccio's fingerprints were all over them. Our little friends were clearly involved in the murders there. They've been charged and they'll eventually come up before the magistrates. No question about it, Chief. We've got them cold. These are the bar-tabac murderers.'

That evening, as they ate a celebratory dinner at Luigi's, Madame brought up the question that was in the minds of all of them.

'What happens now?' she said. 'Do we all go home at the end of the week, or do we take a little extra holiday at the Vicomte's expense – and the Duponts', I might add – to make up for the time we've lost.'

Pel was silent for a moment. 'There's no rush,' he said.

This was unlike Pel. He was normally as restless as a flea and she couldn't imagine, any more than De Troq' could, what he would do with himself now that the thing had been sorted out.

'Well,' De Troq' said. '*I'll* have to go. That's certain.'

'Not yet,' Pel said and De Troq's eyebrows rose.

'Oh?'

'I don't think we've finished yet.'

'But we've got them all, Patron.'

'I wonder if we have.'

'Don't you think we have?'

'There's one thing we haven't found out yet. And that's *why*?'

'Why?'

'I thought,' Madame Pel said, 'that the taxi-driver was killed because he'd learned that those three were responsible for killing the six men in Marseilles and the doctor because he'd guessed.'

'Yes,' Pel agreed. 'That's true, but nobody's found out yet *why* those three killed the six in Nice. We've got a pretty shrewd idea, mind. Smuggling. And, after all, you don't kill six men for a smuggled typewriter, a radio or a bicycle. For that matter, nor do you kill for wool, wood, or wheat, watches or scientific or optical instruments. These days drugs are the biggest thing there is. The profits are enormous and to some people well worth taking a risk for. Marseilles has always been a good inlet into France. We also,' he pointed out, 'haven't yet found out who told Riccio he'd been seen and who was the third man in the boat. It's my guess they're the same persons.'

With some reluctance, Pel faced the paper work again. A new brigadier and a new constable were due to arrive in two days time and the rest of the policemen on the island, having seen what had happened to Beauregard, were very much on their toes and eager to help. Doubtless, Pel suspected, they too had taken bribes in their time – it was hard not to, when the man at the top was doing it – but he had a suspicion that they'd received a nasty jolt and wouldn't do it again.

By the afternoon, however, he had been reduced to a foul temper by the number of forms he'd had to fill in, and was just staring at the desk and wondering sourly if he dared light another cigarette because he'd already, he felt sure, smoked half a million since breakfast, when De Troq' put his head round the door.

'Someone to see you,' he said.

'I'm too busy to see anyone.'

'I think you'd better see this type.'

It turned out to be Lesage.

'Well?' Pel snapped.

It was ungracious of him, he knew, but he wasn't feeling in a particularly gracious mood.

'I've got something to show you,' Lesage said.

'Such as what?'

'You'd better come and see. I left it where it was because I thought that's what you'd want.'

Pel glanced at De Troq' then back at Lesage. 'Where is it?' he asked.

'At that cottage belonging to the Vésins. We've just found it.'

Pel glanced again at De Troq' and rose to his feet. 'Let's go,' he said.

Lesage drove them in his battered car up the slope from the town. The smoke had stopped by this time and a lonely fireman, whom Pel recognised as Desplanques, was poking about among the cooling remains of the cottage.

'There wasn't much that could be saved from inside,'

159

Lesage said. 'It's all charred wood and fabric. The garage just contained a few scorched tools, a rusty lawn mower and something else. You'd better have a look.'

He led them round the back of the house and kicked open the scorched door of the garage. Inside among the fallen timbers, they immediately realised why he'd considered what he'd found was important. Lying in a corner where it had been hidden by boxes which had been yanked aside by the firemen was a Rapido Miniature coffee machine, blackened by smoke, its red paint blistered by the heat. Lesage moved several boxes to produce two more.

'Coffee-making machines?' Pel said. '*Three* of them? Why three? Why would an elderly couple from Nice want three coffee-making machines? And why hide them? Contact them, De Troq'. Let's hear what they have to say.'

By means of the radio, they learned that the Vésins knew nothing of any coffee-making machines. They didn't possess even one, let alone three.

'Were they Oudry's, Patron?' De Troq' asked. 'He had a key. The Vésins admit he did. Is that what he was looking for?'

'Why not?' Pel said. 'I suspect we know now who passed on to Riccio the information that he'd been seen by Caceolari. Who was with Riccio that night? Maquin and one other. The Robles woman knew Caceolari had seen guns because he told her so. Caceolari's wife also knew he'd seen something because he told her. But Madame Caceolari didn't know it was guns. And she and the Robles woman weren't in contact with each other. So the only other person who could know anything would be Caceolari's sister, Madame Oudry. Madame Caceolari went to see her more than once a week.'

Pel was silent for a while. 'Oudry was a drinking friend of Riccio's and if Madame Caceolari mentioned to her sister-in-law something about Riccio being seen with two other men that night they came back from the mainland, it's not unreasonable to imagine that Madame Oudry would mention it sooner or later in all innocence to her husband. And, if Oudry *were* the third man, then he'd immediately pass it on to Riccio and Maquin because it was obviously essential that Caceolari's tongue had to be stopped. And, if you remember, when Riccio's boat came back that night, it dropped the guns then went off north. Of course it did. It went to Biz to drop Oudry. It begins to look as if Riccio and his friends were not only prepared for a small sum to bump off the people who were cheating Tagliatti but that they were prepared to cheat him a little themselves – free. I suppose it's what's known as honour among thieves. Bring him in.' He paused. 'And while we're at it,' he ended, 'we might as well do the job properly. Just nip along and bring in our friend, Billy the Burner. You know who I mean.'

With Oudry in a cell in the police station and Pel once more filling in the necessary papers, De Troq' waited in Hell's Half-Acre with a drink in front of him. Eventually he saw a figure on a blue two-stroke motor cycle coming along the harbour from the garage. He rose and waved a hand and the blue motor cycle stopped. On the rear pillion was strapped a tightly-fastened can.

'What's in that?' he asked.

The rider smiled. 'Paraffin,' he said.

'What for?'

'Madame Ferre. She lives at the back of the Port.'

'Why can't she fetch it herself?'

'She fell and broke her ankle. I help Lesage in my spare time. My round only takes me to the middle of the afternoon. Then I help him. Everybody does two jobs here.'

'You've done several, though, haven't you?' De Troq' said.

'Several what?'

'Several jobs. Since we arrived, that is, and God knows how many before. It was you who set that cottage on fire last night, wasn't it?'

'Me? No.'

De Troq' smiled. 'Apart from the estate agent who handles the lets and the owners themselves,' he said, 'I can't think of anyone who would know better than the postman when the cottages are empty. You've been going at it a bit too enthusiastically just lately, my friend. Whose house was it to be tonight?'

21

Pel was in a thoughtful mood as he walked to the booking office for the ferry to Calvi.

The ship was already in, and already crowded with the islanders who were clambering on board carrying suitcases, cartons, baskets, bags, even the inevitable crate of chickens. Gnarled brown hands pushed screwed-up bundles of notes through the hatch at the booking clerk and he was already in a bad temper as he tried to peel them apart.

'Is this how you always carry your money around?' he growled at one boy.

'Yes,' the boy answered cheerfully. 'The tighter you screw them up, the less room they take in your pocket.'

Pel waited until the queue had disappeared before approaching to ask what time the boat left.

'Ten o'clock,' the clerk said. 'Arrives four o'clock.'

'Every day?'

'Every single one.'

'And return?'

'They cross. The Calvi ferry arrives here seven-thirty in the evening. Leaves Calvi at one-thirty.'

'Eat on board?'

'Drink, too. I don't recommend the meals, mind. Judging by the taste, they're prepared by a type who probably has one arm, no sense of smell and cross eyes. The wine tastes like a paperhanger's adhesive. If I have to go I take a sandwich and a bottle of beer.'

The clerk was obviously a cynic.

Returning to the Dupont house, Pel found Madame in the kitchen preparing dinner in a state of bemused delight.

'The Duponts came,' she said. 'They'd heard about the arrests and wanted to know when we'd be leaving. I told them not yet. They seemed a bit down in the mouth.'

162

Pel smiled. 'We're going to Calvi tomorrow,' he said.

'By boat?'

'Of course.'

Remembering how little he'd enjoyed the last boat trip, Madame was, to say the least, suspicious but she was getting to know her Evariste Clovis Désiré, so she said nothing and quietly made her preparations.

Seeing De Troq' off to the mainland with Oudry, Babin and a large carton containing the three coffee machines they'd found, they caught the ferry the following morning. By the grace of God, the sun was out but though the sea was like a millpond Pel still managed to feel queasy.

Most of the time he sat deep in thought. Madame didn't interrupt him but sat happily alongside him, knitting and humming to herself.

> *'Rosalie. Elle est partie*
> *En chemise de nuit*
> *Dans un taxi –* '

The banality of the words suddenly penetrated Pel's thoughts.'Where did you learn that?' he demanded.

She gave him a wide contented smile. 'I don't know. I pick them up.'

He disappeared behind his face again as his thoughts took over once more. Madame held up the knitting.

'Do you like it?' she asked. 'It's a sweater for you to wear in the evening when you've finished work.'

He tried to sound enthusiastic but he knew he'd never wear it. Whatever the time of day, Pel always remained properly dressed, usually in a suit. Normally it looked as though it had been slept in, though now he was married, he thought, his clothes would be pressed and he'd become the pride and joy of the Police Judiciaire. Perhaps, even, the Tailors' and Cutters' Association would give him a prize as the best-dressed policeman in France.

'It'll help you to relax,' Madame added. 'In Monaco and St. Trop' men even have play clothes.'

Pel nodded. He was already learning to listen with one half of his brain and think with the other. 'My play clothes,' he observed, 'are when I take my jacket off.'

The sun was hot as the ferry came alongside at Calvi and the first thing that seemed to be necessary was a drink. They took it in a bar overlooking the sea and, to Madame's surprise, Pel settled for a coffee.

'Not a beer?' she asked.

'I fancy a coffee,' he said.

She didn't argue, especially when she noticed that the coffee came from one of the Rapido Mini machines. The barman placed it on the table and allowed them to help themselves.

'Barmen seem to be growing incredibly lazy these days,' Madame complained. 'Everybody seems to have these things.'

It didn't escape her notice that Pel became heavily involved in a conversation with the barman and very quickly discovered which of the neighbouring houses was the Vicomte's. It was a wide-verandahed place with frescoed walls surrounded by pines and cypresses and it had its own small jetty running out into the bay.

'Very useful for getting ashore quickly,' Pel commented.

It also didn't take him long to find out the name of the local agents for the coffee machines.

'Guardaluccis',' the barman said. 'Just up the road here. The name's on the door. They'll sell you one. Knock a bit off, too, if you ask nicely.'

Madame followed Pel up the dusty road. She felt a bit like the wife in the Jacques Tati film, *Monsieur Hulot's Holiday*, but she didn't complain. She suspected that her Pel was up to no good and she was intrigued to find out what it was.

They were met at the door of Guardaluccis' by a bright young man in horn-rimmed glasses who agreed to show them round. There were several benches and on all of them girls were assembling the red machines. Along the benches were red-painted panels, nuts, screws, wires, heating elements and tubes.

'It's the same principle exactly as the big machines,' the bright young man said.

'These days I notice remarkably *few* big ones,' Madame Pel said tartly. 'Especially in restaurants. They all seem to be little ones like these that you have to operate yourself.'

The young man smiled. 'Well, they *have* rather caught on,' he admitted. 'It's the thing these days to let people help

164

themselves. It makes them think they're getting more for their money and does away with the extra help that's needed.'

'Where are they made?' Pel asked.

'Sicily. Place called Ferno, close to Catania. Do you know Sicily, Monsieur?'

Pel didn't and he was too interested in other things to enquire about it. 'How do they get here then?' he asked. 'Through Genoa?'

'They come up the length of Italy and pass across the Tyrrhenian from Piombino to Portoferraio in Elba and from there to Bastia. And from there to the mainland of Europe. Switzerland and France chiefly, though we're selling them now in the north – Holland, Belgium, even a few in Scandinavia.'

'So why are they *here*?'

'For Southern France, Monsieur. They come over the mountains to us by ordinary tourist bus. Just cartons of parts placed among the tourists' luggage. It's cheap. They're not big or heavy and they travel for practically nothing. We assemble them here and send them to Monaco, Cannes, Toulon, and other places.'

'But not to Marseilles or Nice?'

'No, Monsieur. For Nice and Marseilles they go via the Ile de St. Yves. Our agent for that area's the Vicomte de la Rochemare. He buys other things from this island and was able to get the concession without trouble.'

They spent the night at a hotel recommended by the young man who sold the Rapidos. The menu wasn't much to write home about and there was nothing to do after dinner except watch the television. It turned out to be *Dallas*.

'I've seen this one,' Madame said. 'What's on the other programme?'

The waiter grinned. '*Dallas*, Madame,' he said. 'We get our programmes from France, Italy, Switzerland, Spain and Austria, and they all show *Dallas*. You can get it almost every night of the week here.'

Madame Routy, Pel decided, would have loved Corsica, and it seemed less wearing to go for a walk by the harbour where, Madame noticed, Pel seemed inordinately interested in the Vicomte's house.

The next day was spent in a hired car exploring the mountains where the flowers were running riot. It was hot and they found a small farm where they had an excellent lunch with a local wine at what Pel considered a give-away price, walked together under the trees, cooled their feet in a mountain stream, then drove back to Calvi, turned in the hired car and caught the afternoon boat back to the Ile de St. Yves.

As they returned in the cool of the evening, the sun like a bronze ball in the sky, Pel was quiet. His wife sat alongside him in the sunshine, saying nothing. She had discovered that when Pel was unnaturally silent it was a good thing for her to be silent too. She didn't mind. She admired him for his sense of duty and the intensity with which he tackled anything, feeling that if he tackled his marriage with the same intensity it had a good chance of working.

De Troq' was waiting with the Duponts' Peugeot and as they drove to Hell's Half-Acre for a drink, he nodded to three holidaymakers with knapsacks, tents and hiking boots who were just preparing to leave the square on hired motor cycles.

'Ledoyer, Berthelot and Morel,' he said. 'It was decided in Nice and Marseilles that we're on to something. Riccio and his pals still aren't talking and they're asking themselves in Nice the same questions we're asking here. They thought we should have a little hired help.' He indicated a large envelope. 'All in here, Patron,' he went on. 'Forensic Lab's report on those three coffee machines we found. It was just as you thought. They'd been sealed with wax. To stop the smell. There were still traces of it on the joints of the upright column.'

'Right,' Pel said. 'We'll deal with it tomorrow.'

De Troq' didn't argue. He'd returned from the mainland with a bunch of female tourists from England and since he was brisk, arrogant, handsome, and had a title – *and looked as if he had* – one of them had fallen for him hook, line and sinker.

Most of the following morning was spent telephoning Inspector Maillet in Marseilles. Still nobody was talking but Madeleine Rou had told Maillet that she thought the heroin she'd been trying to hand over had come from the Ile de St. Yves. By this time it seemed obvious that this was the case and, driving the Duponts' car into the mountains, they found the three Marseilles cops sitting outside their tent. Morel was pressing wild flowers in a contraption made of plywood. He explained that he was doing it because his wife used them to make postcards and was making quite a nice line of it for the gift shops, thank you. It cost him nothing and the results helped to buy the baby a new bib. He'd worked with the drugs squad and knew his facts.

'Heroin comes from opium,' he said. 'It's made into a morphine base and turned into heroin by the buyer. It needs a lot of expertise and no two chemists get the same degree of purity. But wholesalers demand high standards because they like to stretch it for extra profit with milk powder, sleeping pills and strychnine, and a gram of heroin in the street can contain no more than ten per cent of the original pure heroin. And since it's never known what the buyer's used to stretch it, too much can mean death. Heroin does nobody any good but the dealer.'

On the return journey to the Vieux Port, they discussed the ramifications of the case.

'Tagliatti's in it, that's for sure,' De Troq' said. 'And *he* knows Rambert. I dare bet *he's* also involved in that murder of Boris de Fé two years ago and De Fé was involved with this guy Hoff over that phoney insurance and the group of petrol stations he got in Paris.'

'There's Hardy, too,' Pel reminded him gently. 'The junior minister in Paris.'

'*And* the type he bought the yacht at Ste. Marguerite from. They're all in it together. But there's something missing, Patron. We can still only guess. We have everybody in the scenario but Rochemare, when he *ought* to be in. And if he *is* in it, then why did he bring *you* into the case? That was *his* doing and if he *is* involved, he must have known you'd turn something up.'

'He probably had to bring me in, Pel pointed out. 'Because *I* was the one who found Caceolari. A senior police officer. If I'd not been a cop or even if I'd been an unknown cop he might have hushed it up. But he knew I'd not let it rest, so he had to put on a show and hope nothing would get past all those silent island tongues.' Pel paused. 'Not much did, did it?'

*

167

Nelly had cooked the evening meal and, because De Troq' was coming, she'd decorated the table with flowers. She'd borrowed the Duponts' Renault to go into the hills to collect them and they surrounded the candlestick and the centre of the table and each place setting. She'd cooked a joint of veal and a tarte aux fraises, and produced one of the Vicomte's bottles of wine; though the flowers tended to get in Pel's way when he liked plenty of room for his eating, he couldn't help complimenting her on them.

'They're magnificent,' De Troq' agreed and she blushed with pleasure.

'I often did it at the château when they had a dinner party,' she said. 'The housekeeper said I was good at it. The Baroness de Mor once got me to go to the mainland to do it for a special party she was giving.'

'I've heard of Baron de Mor,' Pel said. 'Who is he?'

'A friend of the Vicomte's. Well, not so much him as his wife, the Baroness. She often came. She was the Vicomte's friend really.' Nelly looked disapproving. 'A very good friend. She often stayed at the château on her own. Her daughter, Isabelle, was at school with the Vicomte's daughter, Elodie, and she was a bridesmaid when Elodie was married. Actually, the party was for her and it went off very well. She was delighted with the way things went. She was the one who gave me this.'

She took off the gold bracelet she wore and handed it to Madame who read out the inscription. 'To Nelly with thanks. Isabelle Addou.'

Pel sat up abruptly. His mind was like a filing system and this was also a name he'd heard before somewhere. 'Addou?' he said. 'Addou? I know that name.'

'Yes,' Nelly said. 'She married a financier called Addou.'

'Who did?'

'The Baroness de Mor's daughter, Isabelle.'

De Troq' was sitting up, too, now. 'Addou,' he said in a choked voice. 'The type Hardy bought that boat from, Patron. At Ste. Marguerite.'

'Let me have a look at that!' Pel took the bracelet and studied it then he looked hard at Nelly. 'And who did the Vicomte's daughter, Elodie, marry, Nelly? Anyone we know?'

'I shouldn't think so.' Nelly shrugged. 'A man called

Marcoing. But it didn't work. She didn't have a lot of luck and she wasn't a very happy girl. She divorced him within three years and married the Comte de Jarnoux.'

'And does that marriage work?' Madame asked.

'I don't think so. Not really. She often talked to me. She was often lonely. She was the only child and her mother was always away.' Nelly was at her informative best. 'They were married here on the island. Quietly, of course, because of the divorce. My boy friend says he gets his name in the papers a lot because he's in politics. She met him through the Addous. He was a friend of Monsieur Addou's.'

She realised Pel and De Troq' were staring at each other and stopped dead. 'Have I said something wrong?' she asked. 'Have I been giving away secrets when I shouldn't?'

'Name of God, no!' Pel said briskly. 'Sit down, Nelly. Have some wine and tell us more about this Comte de Jarnoux. What else do you know?'

Nelly looked puzzled. 'Nothing, Monsieur. Only about the wedding.'

'Did your boy friend say whether the Comte de Jarnoux's rich?'

'Oh, yes. Very rich. Richer than her first husband. He has a cement works in Picardy somewhere. Near Amiens, I think. But we knew that because all the cement for the new harbour and the hotel came from there. They say Rambert arranged it. They say he made a lot of money.'

'Judging by the amount they used,' Pel said, 'I'd be surprised if he hadn't. Was the Vicomte involved in it?'

'Elodie told me they did a lot of business together. She also told me she didn't think the marriage to the count would work either and was thinking of divorcing him, too. She said she could afford it because her father had left her a lot of property on the island. I thought she meant the château but she said it was in addition to that, so it must have been the hotel and a few other things. At Muriel, I thought.'

'Bit of a hypocrite, our Vicomte, isn't he?' De Troq' said. 'Supporting the islanders on the one hand, and on the other hand part of a financial group developing the place against their interests. If he lied about that, perhaps he lied about a few other things, too. They must have been making a fortune between them. Perhaps even one each.'

'Oh, I don't think the Vicomte needed money,' Nelly said earnestly, the habit of loyalty strong in her. 'He always had plenty. I don't think the Comte de Jarnoux did either, for that matter. He had plenty long before they built the harbour. His family owns a timber company in Marseilles and another company in Perpignan. Sulphur or something, my boy friend said.'

Pel had sat bolt upright. 'What was that you said?'

'Sulphur.' Nelly looked worried. 'Are you sure I've not said something wrong?'

'No, no! On the contrary, you've just produced a link we've been trying to find for days.'

'Is it involved with your enquiries, Monsieur?'

'It could be.' Pel looked at De Troq'. 'I don't suppose your boy friend told you about bribes being pushed around, too, did he?'

De Troq' was looking uncertain. 'Patron, it can't be,' he warned. 'We've been looking for the link all this time and here it was, on our own doorstep all the time. Coincidences don't come like that.'

'Sometimes they do.' Pel took a sip at his wine and, with a guilty look at his wife, treated himself to an extra cigarette – extra to the extra one he'd just had. 'When I was a young cop I knew a girl who was taking a holiday in Paris when she was picked up by a type for whom she fell pretty heavily. She agreed to go away with him but as she was walking down the Champs Elysées with him a car that had been hit by a taxi went out of control, mounted the curb and killed him. She was still sobbing her heart out when a cop who'd appeared told her she was the luckiest girl alive. The guy was Alain Delacroix. You might have heard of him. White slaver. His technique was to get girls to go away with him. After that nobody ever heard of them again. What's more interesting is that the car was driven by her brother, who didn't even know she was in Paris. If that isn't a coincidence, I've never seen one. Perhaps this is another.'

When the police boat appeared again three days later, in the cabin with Inspector Maillet was a man from the Paris fraud squad investigating Hardy, the deputy to the Minister at the

Bureau of Environmental Surveys. Hardy was still wriggling to great effect and difficult to pin down, but, though he produced new and ingenious explanations every time the fraud squad produced incriminating documents, they were not letting go.

'Sulphur,' Mailett said at once. 'You were dead right. Hardy's been receiving subsidies that should have gone to private producers of the stuff, to compensate them for holding on to their stocks for government use. They'd been earmarked for industry in the event of an emergency.'

'But – ' the fraud squad man took up the story ' – he hasn't been paying them and instead, in fact, has been accepting cash from one or two producers – including some you'll know – to say nothing about what's been going on. And while the subsidies weren't paid and the producers didn't hang on to their stocks but sold them for profit, other poorer quality sulphur that was being bought by the government for something else entirely and paid for by an entirely different department, was being hived off to make up the missing stocks.'

'It sounds complicated.'

'It's intended to be complicated. It *has* to be complicated. That's how they work. And these days they're helped by the speed of communications and travel. A man can set up a company here in the morning and be setting up another in New York the same night. Fraud's always with us. Because, for one thing, the public loves the crooks. It laps up their lavish life styles and human greed makes fraud easy.' The fraud squad man had a distinctly cynical attitude to his fellow human beings.

He turned over a few sheets of paper from his brief case and looked up. 'The contracts Hardy arranged,' he went on, 'are quite illegal. Some of the profits went into a new company in which he had an interest, Addoujarnoux du Sud – the directors should be fairly obvious – and the sulphur which was being stored in place of the missing stocks came from the Sulphur Company of Perpignan – at a price considerably less than that with which it was sold to the government. As a result, a tidy sum of money's been going into the accounts of Hardy, Addou, Jarnoux and one or two others such as an entrepreneur by the name of Johann, who runs a firm in

Switzerland, and a type called Hoff, who's involved with Addou in a few other things we're interested in.'

'Such as the murder of a shady financier called Boris de Fé, shot in Marseilles two years ago?'

'Such as the murder of a shady financier called Boris de Fé shot in Marseilles two years ago.' The fraud squad man smiled. 'We think Johann works for Tagliatti and we've noticed also that he represents the Vicomte de la Rochemare as his agent for olive oil and a few other things. The money they got out of the deal's been used to buy shares in a big new plate-glass manufacturing combine owned by a type called Kern, which has recently gone public, so it's been pretty successfully hidden.'

'Any of them glass manufacturers?'

'Not one. They're all money boys. Operators. Manipulators. Clever ones. But not quite clever enough, because we found out what they were up to.' The fraud man sketched a small modest shrug. 'It's getting harder for them, of course, because there are stricter laws and regulations governing financial markets these days. But there are also new investment vehicles and technical innovations and if things have improved for us since Stavisky brought down the government – two governments – in 1934 with his bogus municipal credit bonds, they've also improved for them. No matter how hard we try, there's always another loophole. And it seems Hardy's the boy to find it. He refuses to admit anything, of course, and still claims the money he's been using came, as he claimed originally, from an American friend called Elliott. But Elliott's the guy who put "chic" into chicanery and his activities won't stand much investigation. We'll break them all down eventually. Paris already have Hardy, Addou and Elliott and Perpignan have Jarnoux. Tagliatti, of course, is safe in Switzerland and we can prove nothing on him, while Hoff seems to have vanished to South America. I'm here to pick up Rambert and your friend, the Vicomte.'

Pel sat up sharply. 'Not yet,' he said vigorously. 'Not just yet. I have a little bone to pick with the Vicomte before then.'

22

There was a need for care.

Undoubtedly the Vicomte de la Rochemare's finances had benefitted considerably from the activities of Hardy, Addou, Jarnoux, Rambert and the others. But that didn't mean that *he himself* had worked the deal. There were plenty of people involved in his affairs, including the accountants who acted for his companies, his stockbrokers – and Tissandi.

Tissandi was tall and elegant. So, come to that, was Ignazi. Had they – one of them – or both – been using the Vicomte's name and funds to make themselves fortunes? Like the Vicomte, they were both in the habit of visiting Paris and the mainland regularly on the Vicomte's business, and all three regularly moved about along the south coast of France, into Italy, only forty kilometres east of Nice, to the French islands of Corsica and Elba, and the Italian islands of Sardinia and Sicily. Sometimes their trips took days. Was one of them the mysterious tall man who'd been seen with Hardy?

It was pretty clear that Jean-Bernard Fleurie, who had once worked in the packing department at the château, had been the link between whoever was operating there and Tagliatti. Either Tagliatti had used him to bring in the man who was operating the château end of the line, or the man at the château – Tissandi or Ignazi or the Vicomte – had used him to recruit Tagliatti to get rid of the drugs they were bringing into the island in the japanned boxes. And Doctor Nicolas had guessed what was going on because his own son had died while he'd been on drugs, which was why he'd been so willing to pass on his suspicions to Pel.

Everything began to hang together because Jean-Bernard knew Riccio, and Riccio knew Tagliatti, and Tagliatti must have known that Riccio knew Tissandi. It wouldn't have taken the gang long to realise that some of their profits were going astray. Doubtless it was Riccio, Maquin and Oudry who took the doctored Rapido Minis to the mainland, and, if they'd been putting a few aside for themselves, it wouldn't take *them* long to become aware that some of them, thanks to Jean-Bernard and his friends, were going missing. Jean-Bernard had even compounded his stupidity by boasting of it to Riccio.

A word in the ear of Tagliatti's deputy in Marseilles would give Riccio and his friends the go-ahead at once to remove Jean-Bernard and *his* friends. And that would not only have pleased Tagliatti but would also stop up the small private leak Riccio had organised. And *that* would have meant that, so long as Tagliatti didn't also learn of Riccio's private little fiddle, everybody, apart from Jean-Bernard and his friends, would be delighted with the way things had turned out. All very satisfactory. *Having learned*, however, Tagliatti was doubtless at that moment biting the carpet because of the rotten low-down treachery of faithful followers like Riccio and taking a long hard look at a few more of them with a view to having them bumped off, too. It suited Pel. Anything that gave Tagliatti ulcers and removed a few of his friends saved the police a lot of trouble.

As it happened, Tissandi had just left for the mainland for a few days to attend to some business of the Vicomte's.

'He's using the Vicomte's boat,' Ignazi explained. 'He'll bring the Vicomte back with him. It's faster than the ferry and doesn't break down as often.'

And doubtless, Pel thought, doesn't make its passengers so seasick.

They persuaded Maillet and the fraud squad man to hang on a little longer. It took some doing because they were afraid the news of the arrests in Paris and Perpignan couldn't be kept quiet much longer, but the following day a message arrived to say that Tissandi was back.

'We had him watched,' they were told. 'We're still in the clear. When do you move?'

'This evening,' Pel said. 'He'll be out on the estate during the day. We'll wait until we've got him indoors. He has an apartment at the back of the château. He'll be there.'

*

174

They spent the rest of the afternoon discussing the way things were to go, then they ate an early meal with Madame. Because it was Nelly's day off and her boy friend had arrived on the afternoon boat, Madame had cooked filet aux olives and opened another of the Vicomte's wines. It went down particularly well under the circumstances.

As they finished, they pushed their chairs back. It had been raining a little and a few small puddles lay on the verandah and on the road outside. Madame stared out at the darkness, her face concerned. She had put on a new dress she'd bought at one of the little boutiques by the harbour, and a pair of new and expensive high-heeled shoes in an attempt to make it an occasion, though Pel suspected that the truth was that she was worried sick. It made him feel warm. He hadn't had anybody apart from his squad worry about him for years.

As she stared out, she saw De Troq' on the verandah checking his gun and she looked at Pel in alarm.

'Have you got a gun, too?'

He nodded. 'It's usual.'

'Will *you* be shooting?'

'Not if I can help it. I couldn't hit a pig in a passage.'

'Aren't you afraid?'

'Being afraid's one of the reasons I've survived so long.'

She looked at him in silence for a while before speaking. 'Is it nearly over?' she asked.

'Nearly,' Pel promised.

'Can we go home then?'

'As soon as we've done the paper work.'

'I'm glad,' she said. 'At first I thought it exciting but suddenly I'm not so sure. Besides, at home there's so much to do.' She managed an uncertain smile. 'Ought I to put a bottle of champagne in the refrigerator to celebrate?'

Pel nodded. 'I should make it two,' he said. 'With the boys from Nice, there'll be a lot of us and policemen were never behind the door when it came to drinking.'

As they drove along the harbour, they saw the island's yellow postal van parked near one of the bars. The driver, a new man who had taken Babin's place, was standing alongside it talking to one of the policemen who'd come from Marseilles.

They'd changed the face of the place in the short time

175

they'd been there, Pel decided. Especially considering that he'd only come for his honeymoon. Still – a half smile crossed his face – on the Ile de St. Yves, everybody did two jobs, didn't they? Even, it seemed, Evariste Clovis Désiré Pel.

The three Nice cops were waiting for them. They were still in their hiking clothes but Pel noticed that they were ominously patting bulges in their belts and he knew they were armed. As they climbed into the car, De Troq' drove up the hill towards the château. There was nobody about and, stopping some distance away, they dropped the three Nice men among the trees.

'Cover the back,' Pel said. 'In case he tries to run.'

When they rang the doorbell, it was the Vicomte himself who appeared, a thin lanky figure in the shadows.

'Chief Inspector,' he said, particular as always to give Pel his full title. 'Please come in. I was just about to take a walk before it grew too dark. What can I do for you?'

'We wish to see your assembly shop,' Pel said.

Rochemare saw the bleak look on Pel's face and his smile faded. 'But the workers have all gone home.'

'It isn't the workers we wish to see, Monsieur. I imagine you have a set of keys.'

Rochemare glanced again at Pel's face. 'Just a moment,' he said. Reaching for the telephone he picked it up. When it clicked he spoke quietly.

'Ignazi? I'm not to be disturbed. I shall be busy for a while. I've got Chief Inspector Pel here with me. He wants to see the assembly shop.' Replacing the instrument, he reached into a drawer and produced a bunch of keys. 'Please come with me, Messieurs.'

They followed him back to the front door. 'Your car?' he asked.

Pel opened the rear door. The car was full of all the cigarette ends he and De Troq' and the Marseilles cops had smoked, together with a crumpled newspaper and a few toffee papers, even a few crushed wild flowers that had escaped Morel's press. Rochemare climbed in fastidiously. After his own immaculate Citroën it was as if he were climbing into a grubby tumbril to go to the guillotine.

De Troq' drove across the estate, by the broad, asphalted road towards the stables. The place was in darkness but

Rochemare unlocked it and began switching on lights. 'Just what is it you wish to see, Messieurs? The freezers? The packing?'

'The assembly shop. That's all.'

Rochemare opened a door for them and they passed through. In the glare of the electric lights set high up in the ceiling, the place looked bleak. Immediately in front of them was a pile of japanned boxes, alongside them a tea chest, scales, measures and waxed bags.

Pel picked up one of the open tins and studied it, then he bent over the tea chest and sniffed. Plunging his hand into the tea, he felt around before straightening up, Rochemare watched him carefully.

'What are you searching for, Chief Inspector?'

Pel said nothing but gestured at the sealed boxes which stood separately. Picking one up, he sniffed it, then ran his finger round the edge of the lid.

'Sealed with wax.'

Rochemare nodded. 'That's to keep the flavour in.'

'*And* the smell, of course.'

'Of course. China tea is very fragrant.'

'*I'm* not talking about tea, Monsieur,' Pel said. 'Open it, De Troq'.'

Taking out a penknife, De Troq' cut the wax seal and opened the lid. Inside, the tin was full of tea but, dipping his fingers into it, De Troq' brought out a small plastic bag.

Rochemare's jaw dropped. 'What's that?'

'Heroin, Monsieur,' Pel said coldly.

'Here!' Rochemare looked aghast. '*Here!*'

'Here.' Pel moved across to the bench where the Rapido Minis lay. Panels, nuts, bolts, electric wiring, heating panels, and steel tubes lay in neat groups. He picked up several of the pieces then, putting them down again, turned to one of the completed machines. There were several on the bench and Pel studied them carefully, sniffing from time to time.

'These are finished?' he asked.

'Of course. What's going on, Chief Inspector?'

'Are there others? Packed ready for leaving.'

'I don't know.' Rochemare looked bewildered. 'I've no idea. I don't look after this.'

'Who does?'

'Tissandi.'

'Where is he?'

'In his flat, I suppose. Do you want me to send for him?'

As the Vicomte reached for the telephone, Pel's hand slammed down on it. 'Don't touch that,' he said sharply.

It was some time before they found the packaged machines. They were in cartons in another room where a van stood, obviously ready to take them down to the harbour. Six others stood to one side. Pel counted the six carefully then gestured to De Troq'.

'Open them, De Troq'.'

'Chief Inspector, those things have just been packaged ready for sale.'

'Open them, De Troq'.'

De Troq' cut the plastic binding round the cartons with his knife. Taking out a machine from inside he held it up to his nose then held it out to Pel.

'Waxed round the joints, Patron.'

He had the top off in minutes with the Vicomte constantly demanding to know what was happening. Lifting the lid of the machine, he peered inside the cube-shaped upright column, then, pushing his fingers in, from among the wires it contained he produced a long narrow plastic package filled with white powder.

'Two, Patron,' he said, producing a second and laying it on the bench.

Pel turned to Rochemare. 'Do the others also contain them?'

'I've no idea. I don't even know – '

'Open them all, De Troq'.'

Half an hour later they had every one of the machines open and there were twelve long tubular-shaped packages of white powder, the same size and shape as the package found on Madeleine Rou and her friends in the Kit Kat Klub in Nice.

'What is it?' Rochemare asked. 'Is that heroin, too?'

'Didn't you know?'

'Chief Inspector, I don't know what's going on but I ought to warn you that I possess considerable influence – '

It was a mistake. Even now, Pel wasn't certain how involved the Vicomte was in the movement of drugs – or even if at all – but they had plenty of proof that he'd been involved

– even if only through Tissandi and Ignazi – in a little speculation in island land and the granting of permission by the Ministry of Beaux Arts.

'I'm well aware of that,' he said coldly, his intelligence in top gear. 'I'm also aware how well you've used it to your own advantage.' He gestured at the plastic bags. 'It came from Taiwan in the japanned boxes. Doubtless you or someone you employed – Tissandi for instance – knew exactly when they arrived in Calvi because you could see from that house of yours. It was probably even landed there and brought over here in your launch – probably with a handout to Beauregard to look the other way until it was placed in the selected machines to go to the mainland. Probably also in the suntan beds that your organisation imported. *And* the tubular folding chairs and garden furniture. *Most* of what you import seems to be hollow and very useful as containers.'

'Are you accusing me, Chief Inspector?'

'As far as this is concerned, I'm accusing nobody until I know the full facts. As for the other – the influence you boast of and how it's been used – that's another matter and will doubtless be looked into by another department than mine. At the moment, I think we'll go and pick up Tissandi.'

Even as he spoke, Morel, one of the Nice cops appeared in the doorway. He was red in the face and panting.

'Patron,' he said. 'He's not there! The place seemed quiet so, instead of waiting for the word from you, we investigated. He wasn't there. There's a way out through the cellar. He's gone!'

Pel's eyes blazed with anger. 'Where to?'

'The Range Rover's just shot off from the front of the house down the hill. I think they're both in it!'

'Patron!' It was De Troq'. 'The Vicomte's launch! It's faster than anything else in the harbour! They're probably going to bolt to North Africa or somewhere!'

'Let's go,' Pel snapped. 'Morel! Look after this lot!'

Dashing outside with De Troq', they scrambled into the Duponts' Peugeot and De Troq' took off the brake. The vehicle was rolling down the slope under its own weight even before he started the engine. As it roared to life, he let in the clutch and they shot out of the huge wrought-iron gates and headed down the hill.

The port was lit up. Now that the season was starting, coloured lights had been strung outside all the bars and they could hear the raucous music from a discotheque. The big Peugeot swung off road with a slash of gravel and began to thunder along the harbour, past Riccio's silent darkened premises, past the Duponts' house where Madame waited. It was followed by a few angry shouts from holidaymakers sitting outside the bars and restaurants who were splashed as it shot through the puddles.

Pel was already running for the gangplank as it shrieked to a stop alongside the Range Rover parked near the Vicomte's cruiser. But De Troq' was faster and passed him, shoving him aside to leap on board ahead of him. As their feet thundered on the deck, Ignazi's head popped up out of a hatchway. He had a gun in his fist so De Troq' kicked him in the face like a footballer taking a running kick at goal. The gun shot into the air and plopped into the water alongside while Ignazi, his eyes rolling, blood on his mouth, dropped out of sight.

As De Troq' scrambled through the hatchway after him, he found a sailor standing near Ignazi's crumpled shape. He looked bewildered. De Troq's gun appeared. 'Back up against the wall!' he snapped. 'Where's Tissandi?'

The sailor gave him the contemptuous look of a seafaring man for a landlubber. 'It's not a wall,' he said. 'It's a bulkhead. And Tissandi isn't here.'

For a moment they were nonplussed. Without doubt Ignazi had driven Tissandi from the château to the harbour. The big Range Rover he'd used was there alongside the gangplank with the Duponts' Peugeot. Tissandi ought to have been there, too.

Pel turned to the sailor. 'Where is he?'

'Who?'

'Tissandi.'

The sailor shrugged. 'I don't know. I haven't seen him since we brought him back this afternoon.'

De Troq' grabbed Ignazi and lifted him to his feet. 'What's going on?' he said. 'Where is he?'

Ignazi refused to answer and De Troq' turned again to the sailor. 'What was this one doing here?'

The sailor shrugged. 'He told me to get the boat ready for

180

a long trip. She's fuelled up, of course. She's always fuelled to the top the minute she comes back so she's ready any time the Old Man wants her.'

'Where was she going?'

The sailor gestured at the moaning Ignazi. 'He said something about Corsica and then on to Sicily.'

'On his own?'

'No. Look – ' the sailor gestured ' – can I put my hands down? It makes my arms ache and this, whatever it is, is nothing to do with me. I only run the boat.'

'Put them down,' Pel said. 'Was Ignazi going on his own?'

'No. He said Tissandi was coming along later. With someone else.'

'Rochemare?'

'It might have been. But they wouldn't lock *him* in the cabin, would they?'

'*Is* somebody locked in the cabin?'

'Not yet. But they were going to, I reckon. Ignazi tried the door, locked it and took the key out. I reckon they were going to take somebody with them. Especially as they said I needn't go. I think they weren't coming back.'

'Why – ?' Pel stared about him, puzzled, then he whirled round and yelled at De Troq'. 'The house! Tissandi's gone for Geneviève! Ignazi dropped him off as they passed the house. I'm going up there! Shove this one under lock and key and come after me!'

It wasn't worth starting the car to reach the house and Pel ran as he'd not run for years. Pel's run had always had an old man's sort of action and he normally preferred to let the younger men in his team do it for him, but this time he was at it like an olympic sprinter. He knew exactly what was happening. Hostages! It was the latest element in the game of cops versus robbers. If the big deal you'd planned didn't come off and you found yourself in trouble, you collared a hostage or two – more if possible – and used them to bargain for your liberty. A car to the frontier. An aeroplane to carry you to some country where they weren't so fussy about having criminals within their boundaries.

Damn St. Yves, he thought. Why had they ever come here? He night have known that anywhere outside Burgundy would cause trouble. Next time he had a honeymoon, he'd spend it in Dijon, or Auxerre or Avallon or somewhere sensible like that.

Reaching the house he slowed down, panting. His knees seemed to have come unhooked and he felt as if he'd lost a lung somewhere. Name of God, why did he persist in smoking so much? It left him no wind to handle emergencies. It was all he could do to breathe.

From where he stood he could see the front door of the house and knew that if Tissandi were inside, he couldn't get away without being spotted.

A minute or two later, De Troq' arrived alongside him. 'I tossed him in the police station and told the guy on duty to lock him up, and that if he let him get away I'd have his head. I didn't worry about the seafaring type. He doesn't seem to be part of it.'

Pel gestured. He was getting his breath back now. 'You take the back door,' he said. 'I'll go in through the front.'

As De Troq' vanished, Pel moved into the shadows of the verandah. Turning the door handle slowly, he discovered it was unfastened. Pushing inside, he headed warily for the living room. He almost hoped there'd be a fight and it would be wrecked and all the Duponts' precious objects d'art would be ruined. It would pay them back for enticing them with their lying brochures to this cursed island.

The light was on and, as he crossed the darkened hall, he saw Madame standing by the table. He couldn't see all of her but he knew at once from her position that something was wrong. Then, as he moved closer, he saw Tissandi alongside her, tall and bulky against the light. He had wrenched her arm up behind her and in his other hand he held a Luger 9mm. at her cheek. As Pel stepped into the light, he gestured with his head.

'Throw your gun on the floor.'

Pel stared at Tissandi but he did as he was told. He saw his wife watching him, her eyes appealing, obviously expecting him to do something miraculous to rescue her.

'Stand back,' Tissandi ordered. 'She's going with me. And if you attempt to follow us, she'll be shot and thrown overboard.'

Madame's eyes widened but she didn't move. Pel said

nothing, aware that Tissandi had not yet realised that they'd visited the boat first.

'Move away,' Tissandi went on. 'I'm coming out through the door. But I'll have the gun. Pick it up and hand it to me. Butt first.' The Luger swung towards Pel and, as he reached forward to pick up his gun, he knew exactly what Tissandi intended. He was going to bring the Luger down on the back of his head and braced himself for the blow. But, as he did so, bending with his head at the level of Tissandi's knees, he saw his wife's foot lift. The elegant high-heeled court shoes she'd put on for the celebration she'd hoped for when they returned with it all over and done with, caught the glow of the lights as her foot rose cautiously and Pel moved as slowly as he dared. As she jammed down the high spiked heel on to Tissandi's canvas-clad foot, he gave a strangled yell and Pel immediately dived for his legs.

All three of them crashed in a heap to the floor. Madame screamed and Pel got a foot in his face, but he managed to grab his gun and bring it down on Tissandi's head. Tissandi's gun fell from his hand as he yelled in pain and Pel saw his wife's foot jerk forward and kick it out of reach. Then the door burst open and De Troq' crashed in and fell on top of the struggling heap.

When the shouting and yelling died down, De Troq' had wrenched Tissandi's hands up behind his back and slapped on the handcuffs. Madame was standing by the table supporting herself and, as he crossed to her, Pel was pleased to see the Duponts' whatnot table had been upset and half their objects d'art were lying in pieces. Serve them right, he thought savagely.

His wife gave him a shaky smile as he put his arm round her. 'You all right?' he asked.

'Yes.'

'You sure?'

'I'm perfectly all right. I have a bruise on my hip that'll probably be there when I'm an old woman, but otherwise I'm unharmed.'

Pel kissed her gently and made her sit down. From the Duponts' cupboard he produced the Duponts' brandy bottle and three glasses and, watched by the glowering Tissandi, they toasted their success. Then Pel gestured at De Troq'.

'He's all yours,' he said. 'Put him with the other one and telephone Nice to come and get them in the morning. And keep an eye on them.'

'Patron,' De Troq' said. 'I'll be sitting up all night. I wouldn't trust a damn soul on this island.'

23

By the time they went to bed, Chief Inspector and Madame
Pel were a little light-headed. Though De Troq' and the cops
from Nice were standing guard at the police station, they'd
all called in at various intervals to celebrate with a drink.

As Madame climbed into bed, Pel studied her. 'You're sure
you're all right?' he asked for the hundredth time.

Madame looked at him, her eyes strangely bright. 'Of
course I'm all right,' she said briskly. 'In fact, at the moment
I'm feeling wonderful. They always say champagne is good
after a disaster, a triumph, an operation or going to bed with
someone, don't they?'

Pel turned, startled. There were hidden depths to his new
wife, he decided.

'You're not hurt?'

'I'm stronger than I look. I used to ride, you know, but
I was always falling off. I don't remember suffering much
harm.'

Pel frowned. 'It turned out to be rather more than we
expected,' he admitted. 'From being a simple murder enquiry,
it progressed into a very complicated affair indeed. What
Caceolari saw that night above the harbour was just the tip.
We turned over a few perfectly ordinary stones and all sorts
of surprising things crawled out.' He paused and his frown
grew deeper. 'That was a warning he sent, you know,' he
said.

Madame looked mystified. 'Who?'

'Rochemare. I've thought about it a lot.' Pel indicated
his throat. 'He's in it up to here, I'm convinced. When he
telephoned Ignazi to say he had me with him, he was making
it clear what was happening and telling him to warn Tissandi.
Unfortunately, like Tagliatti, he'll come out of it smelling of
violets. Tagliatti will be watched a bit more closely, of course,

185

but that won't worry Tagliatti. He's got strong nerves. And Rochemare will lose control of the island but I don't suppose that'll worry *him* too much either.'

He paused and did a few mild callisthenics. They wouldn't have strained an eighty-year-old. 'Paris are certain he profited from Hardy's schemes,' he went on. 'But he has so many interests that any profits he's made have been shifted around so often nobody will ever catch up with them. Although all the others are facing charges, Rochemare's claiming he knew nothing about anything and he'll get away with it. After all, he told me Tissandi did all his dirty work. He'll doubtless continue to do so.'

He paused again. 'Tissandi and Ignazi will go away for a few years,' he continued, deep in thought. 'But Rochemare will stand by them and they'll come out a lot richer for taking the can back for him. It's a pity we can never catch the really big boys.'

He paused once more in the middle of his exercises. With his arms outstretched and his knees bent, he looked as if he were about to take off and fly round the room. Madame watched him, amused. 'Still,' he went on, 'we've cleared up a bit of bribery and corruption and the Ministry of the Interior intends that in future this island will not be run as it has been in the past. Name of God, it was feudal!'

'Yes, dear.' Madame was finding it all good thumping excitement but Pel was sometimes inclined to go on too long. 'It seems to me,' she said, 'that you've swept through this island as if you were clearing the Augean Stables.' She looked fondly at her new husband. She was well aware that he was rather an odd character who was likely to develop into a mild eccentric in his old age but, despite the frightening episode that evening, she enjoyed being with him. And the events of the last few days had broken the ice between them as no normal honeymoon could have, so that they were behaving as if they'd been married years instead of only three weeks.

'I'm sorry for everything that happened,' he said. 'I should never have risked it.'

She smiled. 'You saved me from a long trip to Sicily and North Africa – perhaps worse. You. *My* husband.'

'And you saved me from the disgrace of losing my quarry when I had him in my clutch. It's been a terrible three weeks.'

'No,' she protested. 'No, it hasn't!'

'But all the frightening things that have happened!'

'There've been a few other things, too,' she pointed out gently. 'There's been a lot I shall never forget and – ' she lifted her arms as he bent to kiss her ' – I've found a wonderful lover.'

Pel's eyebrows shot up indignantly. Then he recovered quickly and smiled. 'You have?' he managed.

He had very nearly put his foot in it. He had almost said 'Who?'

If you have enjoyed this book and would like to receive details of other Walker mystery titles, please write to:

Mystery Editor
Walker and Company
720 Fifth Avenue
New York, NY 10019